THE
CHARTERHOUSE
OF **PADMA**

ALSO BY PADMA VISWANATHAN

FICTION

The Toss of a Lemon

The Ever After of Ashwin Rao

MEMOIR

Like Every Form of Love

AS TRANSLATOR

Where We Stand
BY DJAMILA RIBEIRO

São Bernardo
BY GRACILIANO RAMOS

PADMA VISWANATHAN

THE
CHARTERHOUSE
OF **PADMA**

a novel

GODINE • BOSTON • 2024

Published in 2024 by
GODINE
Boston, Massachusetts

LIBRARY OF CONGRESS CATALOGING-IN-PUBLICATION DATA
Names: Viswanathan, Padma, 1968-, author.
Title: The charterhouse of Padma / Padma Viswanathan.
Description: Boston : Godine, 2024.
Identifiers: LCCN 2024003310 (print) | LCCN 2024003311 (ebook) | ISBN 9781567928143 (hardback) | ISBN 9781567928150 (ebook)
Subjects: LCGFT: Novels.
Classification: LCC PR9199.4.V57 C47 2024 (print) | LCC PR9199.4.V57 (ebook) | DDC 813/.6--dc23/eng/20240125
LC record available at https://lccn.loc.gov/2024003310
LC ebook record available at https://lccn.loc.gov/2024003311

First Printing 2024
Printed in the United States of America

CONTENTS

P1 Spring to Fall

The crime that is latent in us we must inflict on ourselves.

—J. M. COETZEE, *Waiting for the Barbarians,* also
epigraph to Frederika Randall's memoir, *My Dive.*

The *Amateur Boxer*, by William Ranken: online, its credit tells me it lives at the Salford Museum in Manchester, a place I've never been. But I feel certain I have seen the painting sometime, somewhere: the young man's wiry red hair brushed back from his high forehead in tight waves; his extra-red, cupid-bow lips; the gloves he dangles from one hand alongside a tall crate—where does such a crate exist outside the artist's studio, a dock, perhaps, a stevedore fantasy?— while the other is crossed in front of it, the way some dogs cross their paws as though imitating elegant society ladies.

What actually attracted me to the painting, though? Not the young man's face. Not the shadowed gaze; not the meaty, self-consciously arranged hands; not the slabs of chest and curve of waist. It was the sweater, a turtleneck so thick as to give the appearance of modeling clay. (It wouldn't be out of place on Wallace or Gromit.) The sweater held my eye, because it is chartreuse.

ઝ

Chartreuse, says the *Oxford English Dictionary*'s second definition, is *a shade of colour; a pale apple-green.*

This is the curse of colors: always to be defined in terms of something else. See these definitions for two others:

RED: *Designating the colour of blood, a ruby, a ripe tomato, etc., and appearing in various shades at the longer-wavelength end of the visible spectrum, next to orange and opposite to violet.*
BLUE: *Of a colour of the spectrum intermediate between green and violet, as of the sky or deep sea on a clear day.*

The writers of the *OED* are clearly not insensible of language: it seems it was more important that the definitions be beautiful than consistent in format. But chartreuse was something else before it was a color. It didn't reflect nature, it was concocted out of it.

ɘ♥

The Amateur Boxer: no great mystery why our queer-detection systems ping on seeing an unnamed man rendered in thick impasto. I took our kids to MoMA–New York in the summer of 2018, where only two of the maybe two hundred pieces on display from the permanent collection were by women artists, while the models, apart from commissioned portraits, were almost all women. Why would a man paint another man, a beautiful, young man holding a prop and resting his elbow on a set piece?

To look at him—why else?

Searching under *male painter, female model*, I found articles talking about a related matter I hadn't ever considered: male painters *distracted* by lust for female models, a problem Picasso apparently solved by using his mistresses as models (and vice versa?), while other less bold or more austere men made do with photos.

æ

Chartreuse the color got its name from Chartreuse the liqueur, which got its name from a mountainous region in France, which got its name from the village of Saint-Pierre-de-Chartreuse, where, in 1084, Saint Bruno founded the first Carthusian monastery.

The Carthusians are an enclosed order, isolated in favor of contemplation and prayer: closing all doors to the outer world presumably opens a door to the world beyond.

Whatever or whoever enters such a place is not supposed to leave it.

æ

Why do I want to write about chartreuse? Why do I love it? What is wrong with me that I can't figure that out?

#13 in Maggie Nelson's *Bluets*:

At a job interview at a university, three men sitting across from me at a table. On my cv it says that I am currently working on a book about the color blue. I have been saying this for years without writing a word. It is, perhaps, my way of making my life feel "in progress" rather than a sleeve of ash falling off a lit cigarette. One of the men asks, Why blue? People ask me this question often. I never know how to respond. We don't get to choose what or whom we love, I want to say. We just don't get to choose.

æ

It sounds profound when Maggie Nelson says it, but mostly because it controverts the contemporary Westerner's view of how lives are best run: we choose a profession, choose a spouse, choose whether to have kids. Cultures and peoples that impose these, take away choice, are thought backward, oppressive. We go to war against nations and philosophies that want to take away choice, or that's what we tell ourselves—the Soviets, Daesh—even though "the right to choose" sounds very different in America's domestic battles.

But when I was twenty-three, my parents, who had had an arranged marriage, as had their parents, as had their siblings, as have many of my cousins, people who understood *we don't get to choose what or whom we love*—had they chosen their kids? No. Kids arrive and parents love them—my parents asked if I would like for them to arrange a marriage for me.

How great, sighed my white girlfriends, in the throes of the great fairy-tale uncertainties: Prince Charming? Happily ever after?

But I turned them down. I believed I would get to choose. I believed I chose.

و

And then the earth shuddered, like it was shaking her awake. It did shake her awake, the mattress and her body on her mattress shaken to and fro by the earth's urgency: *Get up! Get up!* Here, in Arkansas, you felt it all the time: long belches (natural gas); the hiccups of an organism forced to swallow too much, too fast.

At least for once it wasn't P's own goddamn body taking her by her own goddamn jugular, squeezing and shaking, trying the exact opposite of waking her up, trying to put her down, down, down. Breathe—

It wasn't that. *For once,* squealed that other voice in her head, and she grimaced, thinking it was going to go off on Mac, but instead, the voice, too, was quiet, luxuriating in the unfamiliar stillness, that exaggerated stillness that doesn't come before a storm, a seizure, a seism, but after, when everything holds its breath waiting to see if it's okay to get moving again.

Mac, beside her, had not awakened. P synchronized her breathing to his, but the sleeping breathe too deep for the awakened. *Too deep for the woke,* she thought, and her lips twitched. If anything, Mac was the woke one, as they both knew. She touched his hand with a finger; it curled around hers at her touch. As she lay waiting to see if she could sense any aftershocks, she detected the demons of her self-loathing creeping in. Her breathing grew still shallower as she began that daily fight.

That was August, nearly six months into the pandemic, Arkansas heat in the middle of its long, high plateau.

꙳

Many Anglophones mistake chartreuse for a purple red. Some people even think it refers both to a red and to a green, a Janus word, a color thought to be itself and its opposite.

Why?

I think they get it confused with puce. In English, the words almost rhyme, two color words from the French, the way our Fayetteville neighbor used to confuse me with the other Asian woman who lives in our neighborhood.

꙳

I was putting away my beloved puce pantsuit and thought, *Puce?* Such an ugly word. And it means flea in French.

No coincidence. That is to say, puce and *puce* did not each evolve from some independent source. (In English, this random evolutionary process has given us bass/bass, carp/carp, temple/temple, as well as true Janus words: cleave, hew, sanction, ravel, bolt.)

Puce is named for the color of flea scat. If you suspect your pet has fleas, use this diagnostic technique: comb the animal and drop the fur in water. Abracadabra, the invisible will be made visible: the little pips will bloom red-purple atop their rafts of fur—the color of blood, their primary ingredient.

ॐ

Once upon a time, the drug dealer living upstairs from me in Montreal adopted a kitten. The kitten would visit me, scratching at the door, napping—a daily migration—in the sunny spot that moved across my floor, learning to bathe itself sitting precariously atop stacks of books.

We lived in a duplex with adjoining, identical purple doors, one that opened straight into my studio, the other onto a staircase up to Thierry's. As he descended into debt, a spiral whose velocity was increased by his unfortunate choice to snort his stock, I lived in terror of one of his sources mistaking my door for his and busting it down with a machine gun. More than once, a knock at his door sent him bolting out through the backyard.

At home, I was getting mysterious bites, mostly around my ankles. I was bitten in my bed, at my desk, at my dining table, invisible intruders attacking me from within my own home. One night, I fled to an all-night café, the Second Cup on Duluth, where I read and snoozed and scratched, basking in the baristas' worried glances.

Eventually, a friend identified the bites: fleas.

Now it was my turn to knock on Thierry's purple door. He and his kitten tumbled out, scratching madly, identically.

෨ඬ

In March, a few days before spring break, the university had shut down during P's graduate translation workshop. Her students had all jumped in their seats simultaneously. They murmured and pointed at their phones and computers: the university had sent out a message. Everyone was to vacate the campus until further notice. P phoned Mac as she left her classroom: he was in his office, assembling his tenure materials; they'd planned to bicycle home together. His phone went to voicemail.

On each story of Old Main, where she taught, all the classrooms gave on to a broad single hallway. The hallway had a single exit onto a landing in a single, light-filled stairwell. From each landing, two staircases descended, to the right, to the left. The stairs parted and met on each floor, at each landing, a kind of folly: it's not as though one staircase was for up or down, and most people took the elevators anyway. She looked out a window from each landing at the view—topiary, fountain, architecture school—nodding to colleagues similarly decamping, exited the building onto yet another landing, with its own two sets of stairs coming off it into a courtyard where Senator J. William Fulbright surveyed his creations from a plinth. The statue showed him in a three-piece suit, its formality offset by his pose—jacket open, hands shoved deep in baggie pants pockets. He wore what looked like farm shoes. P circled him, watching people mill toward their safe places, and was hit by a skirl of blustery spring wind as she got to her bicycle. She stowed her laptop and called Mac again.

"Hey," he answered.

"Hey. Still want to head home together?" She heard noises around him. He had a joint appointment in architecture and business, but his office was in the business college. He felt he had much more in common with the architects. "Where are you?"

It turned out he was at the grocery store, having spontaneously decided, before the announcement even came, to make them dinner. It would surely be a great, no, a grand dinner. She just had to figure out what to do with the meal she had left slow-cooking so as not to have to think about dinner when she got home. She just had to keep that question out of her voice. It was churlish not to be enthusiastic when someone was cooking for you. She'd made that mistake before, didn't want to be that person.

She set her Vans on the ground and steadied herself on her bike rack as she unbuckled her pumps: Fluevogs, wide enough at the toe that she could probably ride in them, but changing only took a sec. She eased the right one off of a little Achilles tendon blister, product of a weird problem this year with missing nylon sockettes. Of all the things.

Mac was dismissive: socks go missing, nothing weird about that. But socks went missing in the dryer—she hand-washed and hung these in their bathroom. It didn't make sense. Not fair that she couldn't wear pumps on bare feet and had to. Not fair that bicycle-compatible business casual was so hard to figure out for chicks. Not fair.

Today, though, her favorite puce pantsuit: pants skinny enough not to need a clip, with a swingy blazer; a little give in the fabric. Badass. Before she got on her bike, she consulted a list on her phone, five phrases from the novel she was translating— five small problems to chew on during the ride home: *il a dragué avec elle*; *elle lui pose un lapin*. Another gust hit her as she cruised across the quad to Carnall Hall, a women's-dorm-turned-inn, its name the butt of every predictable joke, its parking lot the sole bike-friendly campus egress on that side. She realized she wasn't thinking about those phrases, but rather about a pet project, a secret: a loosely linked collection of pensées on her favorite color. No career benefit in it, but she was post-tenure, so who cared? Just a private pleasure. A folly.

A field of green from an Agnes Martin painting clicked across her mind like a slide in a darkened room as she took Arkansas Avenue to Reagan Street to Gregg Street to the Lafayette bridge, and phrases started to form that might evoke that green, as her gears ground forward on the gradual ascent home.

&

Early in the pandemic, just as everyone was starting to understand they would not read all of Tolstoy or learn to make choux pastry while also homeschooling, MoMA put up a webpage of kids' activities, highlighting a portrait by Toyin Ojih Odutola, *Projection Enclave*:

A woman lounges in an overstuffed green chaise, its indeterminate, velvety texture rendered in swathes of lighter green against mossy shadows. I want to say it's a Chagall green, but his green is brighter. And Chagall doesn't have just one green. Also, I have no way to see the work in person and so must rely on various internet reproductions, each slightly different. And yet, I think your idea of Chagall's green—whatever you picture—will be close enough.

The woman is thin, wearing a gray, long-sleeved T-shirt and blue jeans. Her hair is short, a style popular in the seventies that has probably come back in Brooklyn. Her right arm rests alongside her right leg; her left arm is, like its corresponding leg, hooked over the high curved side of descending upholstery. She's unconscious and self-conscious at once: her face is turned away from us, but toward a mirror, so that she gazes back at us from beyond that other frame.

Wait. I thought the woman in the mirror was troubling because she seemed to look past her original. But her body is *also* turned toward us. Her earring is visible in a way it would never be if that were a reflection as we know reflections. These two images are not in sync.

᠎᠎ৡ৵

In 1605, the Carthusian order was entrusted with a document by a nobleman, the way an illegitimate baby might be left at a convent gate. In this case, the bastard was a recipe—of unknown authorship but clearly penned by someone with knowledge of alchemy and the healing arts. Titled *Elixir de Vie Longue*—Longevity Potion—it demands the use of over 130 ingredients, virtually every known herb in the region and then some, for its preparation.

We don't know why the nobleman gave the recipe to the Carthusians, other than that only monks and apothecaries were qualified to decipher medicinal directives. And it wasn't until the early eighteenth century that someone actually tried to make the drink described in the document.

The liqueur emanates a subtle chlorophyllic green, the blend of herbs plucked from the slopes of Chartreuse. Intense, floral, fresh— maybe it didn't guarantee eternal life, but, per the old joke, it helped the drinker not to worry so much about dying.

ৡ৵

La Grande Chartreuse, the monastery, relates its history on its website, in French and in English.

One monk, Brother Charles, would break his hermetic vows to strap liquor bottles on the back of a mule and vend them at markets in and around Grenoble. (Alcohol leads to the breaching of boundaries;

as I write this, counties on every continent are banning alcohol sales to stop the spread of COVID-19.)

Production was stopped when monasteries were disbanded during the Revolution, but a copy of the recipe was kept by a single monk who stayed with the monastery, while the original was smuggled out by another who ended up caged in the Bastille, but passed it to a visiting friend. The friend, unable to brew the potion and thinking religious orders were finished in France, sold it to an apothecary, one Monsieur Liotard. The monk who stayed was elevated into rumor, but even today, knowledge of the recipe is always held by two monks—no fewer, no more.

The monks reclaimed La Grande Chartreuse in 1816, and either M. Liotard's descendants gave them back the recipe when he died, or his widow, perhaps suffering her own postwar privations, sold the recipe back to them. History is murky on this (as on so many things), but apparently from 1840 the monks churned out both the green elixir and a yellow version. These two colors, in their two bottles, side by side, look particularly sublime. (There was also, for a generation or two, an oxymoronic white Chartreuse—like Mocha Dick, the albino whale, it was well loved in its way, but not destined to last.)

Just ahead of the 1905 separation of church and state, however, France nationalized the distillery, selling it to private investors and kicking the monks out of the charterhouse. Reassembling in Spain, they resumed production, giving their liqueur the nom de guerre Tarragone since their own name was legally off-limits.

When, in 1929, the stolen French operation went belly-up—imagine the monks giggling into their sleeves at the karmic justice—friends of the Carthusians bought it back for them, just ahead of a 1935 landslide that destroyed the distillery.

They rebuilt, once more.

ҽ♭

Toyin Ojih Odutola, *Projection Enclave*: uncanny. Beyond the subject's reflection (which is not a reflection), there are two more frames: a round one set high up, which surely is a mirror, reflecting some indeterminate gray bands, and a rectangular one, perhaps a window, framing palm fronds sprouting in sepia light, reminiscent of backdrops in colonial-era commercial studios.

The women—I must refer to them in plural now—are not twins. They are not sitting on two chairs separated by a doorway. What we see through the looking glass, I'm sure of it, is our subject herself— maybe in another place, simultaneously; maybe this place, in another time.

The pose of the one closest to the viewer now looks to me like it's been struck by a puppeteer, the strings connected to her elbow and knee lifted by a great hand in the cosmos.

Or maybe lifted by her counterpart: Ewers and Rye's *The Student of Prague*, or, better, Jordan Peele's *Us*, in two dimensions.

But the longer I look at her counterpart, the more it seems she knows something that the woman in the foreground did not. Maybe she's poised to help her; maybe she already has. Like Tic, in *Lovecraft Country*, traveling through time to the Tulsa Massacre to be the shining stranger-savior his father will always remember. Like Kat seeing (but not recognizing) herself, diving from the boat in *Tenet*. How optimistic to think science might grant us a means to rush through time and space to our own rescue.

ҽ♭

The apothecary Liotard, who had by chance acquired the Chartreuse formula amid the clouds of revolution, never manufactured the elixir. He did, however, dutifully reveal the recipe to Napoleon in 1810, in response to a decree: formulas of all secret remedies in France were to be submitted to the imperial government, as part of an effort to stem the age-old practice of quack profiteering.

Proprietary remedies, a.k.a. *remèdes secrets*: neither officinal (standard preparations kept in stock by apothecaries) nor magistral (specially compounded according to physician's prescription), but instead privately owned, a bugaboo of enlightened physicians, a parallel pharmaceutical industry driven by mountebanks, charlatans, and entrepreneurial doctors developing and profiting from their own concoctions, syrups, and powders.

This long administrative war on secret remedies ultimately failed because it fell afoul of stronger competing values: property rights and rights of free trade and enterprise. Inventors had the right to profit from their patents. As medical historian Matthew Ramsey put it: "Property rights triumphed over the right to health."

Adam Gopnik, writing about therapy in the age of COVID-19 in a June 2020 *New Yorker* article, quotes one therapist for whom doing virtual therapy means spending all day forced to look at herself.

No, that's not quite right. It's worse: *Suddenly you're seeing yourself seeing your patient, and it's disconcerting to say the least,* says the therapist. *"I look like that?"*

In other words, the problem wasn't looking at herself. It was confronting how she looked to others.

This is not an entirely new issue in analysis, says Gopnik, quoting Freud from a footnote in *The Uncanny*:

I was sitting alone in the compartment of a sleeping car, when, following a sudden jolt of the train, the door to the adjoining toilet opened and an elderly gentleman in a bathrobe, wearing a bonnet on his head, stepped into my sleeper. Assuming that he had confused the two doors as he was leaving the toilet and had mistakenly entered my compartment, I leapt up to explain the situation, but immediately had to recognize, to my chagrin, that the invader was my own image, reflected in the mirror of the door to the toilet. I still remember that I found the appearance deeply displeasing.

Gopnik's takeaway is that *the uncanniest thing an analyst can experience is himself.* He's wrong. The uncanniest part of the story is the time delay: Freud's reflection entering, after which Freud leaps up to explain. Encountering one's reflection is perhaps unpleasant; encountering one's reflection in the midst of its independent perambulations—*that* is uncanny.

Seeing your reflection's gaze directed elsewhere—*that's* uncanny.

In front of their house, she checked the mail. Aakash would be home—it was his early release day—and Deepa at a friend's. No message from their schools on her phone, so presumably they weren't closed yet? Her prediction was they would be soon—parents had been applying pressure—but it was more complicated with kids. School closures implicated the whole family.

She stowed her bike, came in the kitchen. The house was eerily quiet but everything was eerie just then, the wind, the news, the being home in the middle of the afternoon.

"Hello?" she called.

Aakash wasn't in the living room and neither was his computer, which was odd because he always wanted to be on his computer when he got home and he wasn't allowed to have it upstairs. She went up and knocked on his door.

"Yeah?"

"What's up, honey?" She subtly tried the knob—locked.

"Just changing."

"Changing?"

"I spilled something on my pants."

She positioned herself in the kitchen. He descended empty-handed, made small talk. Later, he wouldn't answer when she asked him casually where his computer was. Later, she would catch him sneaking it downstairs in a laundry basket. Later, she would learn what he'd been doing with it up there.

For now, though, she sat in the kitchen, accepting that there was no way to avoid the anxiety filling her veins like formaldehyde from multiple drips. She sent comments to her students, especially those whose work had not yet been workshopped; she read the news, Northern Italians and Wuhanese dropping like flies. (What caused flies to drop in such large numbers that it became a saying? The only time she had seen such a thing was in a café, former Czechoslovakia, with hot lights hung at eye level above each table so that small flies kept literally crashing and burning, the little Fokkers falling onto their thick white slices of knedlíky. But surely that was a bit too specific to serve as a source for an expression in English?)

She thought about how to teach the next day's class—twentieth and twenty-first century Francophone lit in translation. Should she cancel? But she had known all week that she might need to switch to online teaching, and she was pretty sure she knew how. Up next: Mauricio Segura's *Côte de Nègres/Black Alley*. God, she loved her job. She loved her job more than her kids. No, don't even think that. They weren't comparable, and you didn't need to choose, even if it felt like you did. Every minute, she felt like she was choosing between them. And the job was, on balance, not that this was quantifiable, but if it were, the job was more consistently rewarding. The rules were clearer. All you had to do was think critically and be available and the rewards poured in: emotional rewards! pecuniary rewards! No money in motherhood, though it had sweet moments. But that wasn't why anyone became a mother, so, again, stop comparing.

What would happen if Mac's tenure bid failed? Was she allowed to think that? So brilliant, Mac, a square peg, like all brilliant people. He hadn't exactly said he was worried, but others were worried for him: a business-school colleague (who was also the friend of a friend, and also the parent of a child in Deepa's grade—in Fayetteville, you were connected to any person worth knowing by at least three vectors) had expressed concern when it came up in casual conversation between them a few months earlier. "He's not publishing," she'd said.

It was a drinks thing at Carnall Hall, a celebration of faculty achievements, the sort of event she seemingly got an invitation for every other week, like there were dedicated members of the dean's (and provost's and chancellor's) office for whom this was their sole duty, paging through catering charts and invitation templates, beginning again the minute the last one finished. P kind of loved them: free wine, rather good canapés, and her colleagues, often very interesting. She hadn't made close friends yet through their ten-going-on-eleven years in Fayetteville, but life had been so busy, with young children and the drive toward tenure. Socializing almost took more time and energy than it was worth. Now that her job was secure and the children old enough to stay home alone, she had hopes for girls' nights, date nights, dinner parties.

P's cranberry-brie puff had desiccated in her mouth and she took a pull on her wine as Mac's colleague elaborated: "He's planning to count his consulting gigs. I think," she said, shrugging derisively and scanning the room. "This is a university. Consulting doesn't equal articles. But Mac—he won't go down without a fight." The woman drained her beer bottle, training her gaze along its neck toward P. "Strange guy."

Did she realize she was talking to his *wife*? What was the purpose of this—to prepare her?

That weekend, P tried to tell Mac what his colleague had said.

"Peer-reviewed publications!" Bubbles of spit appeared on his lower lip. "They hire you because you're cutting edge and then they expect you to color in all their little boxes, their little Scantron rectangles. Make sure you use number two pencil, boys and girls!" When Mac went off, it was a proper performance. "Is that where change is going to happen, in the Scantron reader of yesteryear?"

He was a change-maker. A professional feminist. His dissertation had been on how the most widely used brand of office furniture in North America had created neck, back, and hip problems in three generations of aspiring female executives. And they thought it was just repeatedly banging their heads into the glass ceiling. Industrial design, corporate structures, and feminism: this was Mac's niche. He was ahead of his time, sought after. There weren't many white men qualified for this, but there weren't too many women, either, who would actually help your firm to make physical changes to become a better place for women.

The academy was conservative: this was news? The two of them had had some idea what they were getting into: they both did PhDs, after all, and at one of Canada's most venerated institutions, but that was twenty years ago and maybe every generation thinks more has changed than turns out to be the case.

Later that spring, she would dream that her house came unmoored in an earthquake and slid down the street, stopping when it stuck into the earth where their road ended, where it curved toward downtown and became another street. There was nothing but trees and dirt at that corner: the dream cleaved to a certain real-life logic in that way. It was disconnected in time from her conversation with Mac, or from the earthquake that woke her months after that, but they say dream experiences mirror the real world—if you dream you can't move, for example, it's because your blankets are pinning your legs—so maybe, the night she dreamed that, she felt an earthquake but stayed asleep.

She noted the dream in her diary and didn't think of it again until she found it there a few months after, flipping through in search of another dream. Rereading, she would realize how perfectly, with what terrible perfection, it fit with how she felt: what would happen to them if Mac didn't get tenure? They would be cast off, sliding and wobbling away until they got stuck in a ditch. They would lose the house, with her jewel box of an office on the top floor. And where else could she teach literary translation in a creative writing program? Fewer than ten universities in the entire country, that's where, only maybe two or three of which actually granted a graduate degree in translation. Working anywhere but those few places, she would have to produce scholarly writing or scholarly translations to compete for tenure. (She would have to compete again for tenure.) That wasn't her: she translated novels, books regular people actually read. So: a bit of a square peg herself. But not like Mac. Maybe they could stay? With her income and maybe he could freelance? It was unlikely: there's no way he'd want to stay in the area after being rejected. Plus the stigma. They'd be tugged away and would anyone even miss them.

Tenure was being eroded anyway. Arkansas was unapologetic about its war on the left: Faculty in Fulbright College were told, after the 2016 election, not to post political content on their social media pages during "business hours," that state legislators were watching, hoping to pounce. The memo didn't engage the presumption that most legislators' political sympathies opposed most professors'. A lot of the lawmakers hadn't attended college, though one had fifteen minutes of fame for menacing a fellow shopper in a Walmart parking lot with a gun he had in his trunk. He himself bragged about it on Twitter.

P was never that active on social media anyway, more of a lurker than a poster, but Mac took it as a personal challenge, packing his social media activity in from nine to five, doing more regular work in the evenings. If any legislator wanted proof that professors hewed their podia into soapboxes, they needed to look no further than P's DH. Should they be afraid that these, too—his predilection for controversy, his contravention of the diktat—might affect his tenure bid? They hired Mac because he thought outside the box, but maybe you needed to choose: in or out. Tenure was definitely inside the box.

So *liberté* and *égalité* were not the only principles imported to the United States from France, but also the idea that health—health care, preventions, and cures—was a business opportunity.

Coronavirus vaccine companies to invest in is a trending search as I write this, in June 2020. Health profiteering has pervaded the pandemic from the start (and will likely do so to the finish, though it's far too early to say anything about the finish . . .), when people hoarded masks and hand sanitizer to resell at punishing markups. Caught, they were not even ashamed.

(Editing during the horrific spring 2021 surge in India, I find this in the *New York Times*: *Many public health advocates have called for Western governments to force drug makers to share their own patented processes with the rest of the world. No vaccine producer has done so voluntarily, and no government has indicated that it will move in that direction.*)

৯৬

Although MoMA doesn't specify, *Projection Enclave*, with its luxe, tropically allusive setting and its canny (uncanny) Black subject could be an item from Odutola's series *To Wander Determined*, drawings presented as the private collections of two Nigerian families, one old money, *a noble clan*, the other *a minor aristocratic house whose prominence stems from their work as traders and ambassadors.* The families are connected by the marriage of their sons, in defiance of Nigerian law as we know it. The portraits, the letter, the exhibit are sent forth from an alternative history, a Nigeria that, in the artist's words, *had been left alone.*

A painting must depict the act of seeing, not the object seen, says Patricia Hampl. A commissioned portrait is meant to put viewers in thrall to the sitter's status; the portrait is almost always an homage, unless it's aspirational, and the energy of the artist's gaze should show that. In *To Wander Determined*, fatally stylish men and women look back at the viewer with the confidence and ironic hopelessness—or maybe a gentler thing, the easy cynicism and reflexive evaluative stance—of the rich.

And while the drawings themselves may manifest the artist's

presence from beyond the frame, she also figures within the series as an alter ego: the exhibit comes with an explanatory letter from the families' deputy private secretary, who shares Odutola's name.

è

La Grande Chartreuse, on the French side of their website, says the state was attempting to profit from the monks' recipe and reputation: *En 1810, l'Empereur Napoléon Ier décidant que les « remèdes secrets » doivent être soumis au ministre de l'Intérieur pour être examinés afin d'être exploités par l'Etat.*

The English side curiously omits that motive, saying only, *In 1810, when the Emperor Napoleon ordered all the "secret" recipes of medicines to be sent to the Ministry of the Interior, Monsieur Liotard duly followed the law and submitted the manuscript*—not inserting, as does the French, *to see if the State could profit by them.*

In any case, Liotard's gesture toward pharmaceutical responsibility was wasted: the recipe was sent back stamped *Refused*. La Grande Chartreuse claims this is because it was not considered a secret. The historian Ramsey confirms that many recipes were sent back because they were readily found in numerous print sources, but the recipe for Chartreuse was and still is known only to two people. Maybe it was sent back because it wasn't considered a medicine? The problem—or advantage—to a longevity potion is that you have to drink it on the regular for a long time to figure out if it's any good.

è

Another artist who created stories out of visual sets: William Hogarth. *A Rake's Progress. A Harlot's Progress. Marriage A-la-Mode.* An unpromising start leads to a disastrous end: from dewy hopes to syphilitic sores. Where sex is involved, so, too, the French affliction.

Flaubert, from *The Dictionary of Received Ideas*: SYPHILIS—*More or less everyone has it.*

ॐ

Every secret remedy performs miracles because it is secret; disclose the secret it becomes inert.— Dr. John Bethune Stein, seemingly quoting one Dr. Boyveau-Laffecteur, an inventor, in a 1913 article, "The Rob," about a secret remedy approved by the Royal Medical Society of Paris.

The Rob de Laffecteur revolutionized syphilis treatment: it contained no mercury, just a combination of berries and herbs. (A rob or rub is a sort of fruit decoction, a sweet syrup. The word is apparently Arabic in origin—one source locates it in the *Arabian Nights* of Antoine Galland—but became famous in French from Boyveau-Laffecteur's product.) It was unprecedented, a huge advance in the treatment of the pernicious, widespread malady. Napoleon himself ordered two bottles to be sent to Elba.

Dr. John Bethune Stein gives the recipe, a full list of ingredients and their proportions, untranslated from French: from sarsaparilla and saxafras through guaiacum; roots of white roses and bécatunga; finished with pinches of half a dozen different seeds (carrot, parsley); all in a suspension of rainwater.

It wasn't enough to take the syrup; the patient needed to submit to other processes, like a laxative and an emetic. Some were bled. Climate mattered, so a cure required eight to twelve bottles in France, but only four to eight in warmer places such as Italy.

Assisted by the royal imprimatur and by otherwise adroit marketing—it was given a bump in the mid-nineteenth century by a physician called Giraudeau, who owned various competing robs (including two with identical recipes but different labels)—the Rob de Laffecteur was a strong seller for the next 150 years.

A medical journal at the time of Giraudeau's death said, *He introduced into the practice of medicine the shamelessness and power of impudent and lying advertising,* but those French Royal Commissions predated him, suggesting he was hardly the first to practice *this* art.

இ

Speaking of artists and syphilis: Gauguin. He carried syphilis to Tahiti and passed it on to the teenage girls who posed for him, their eyes filled (just look) with trepidation or curiosity or discomfort or calculation or terror. He never painted syphilitic sores on them, girls of my daughter's age, girls with my daughter's eyes. I think this is a case where we look to see *the object seen,* not *the act of seeing.* Gauguin *was* the French affliction.

Overwhelming, transfixing fear is, in French, une peur bleue, a blue fear, Susan Sontag tells us in *AIDS and Its Metaphors.*

Whereas a sharp retort or rebuke in French is green—*une verte réponse, une verte réprimande*—the adjective slapped out of its customary position after the noun and instead coming first.

இ

Mac blustered into the kitchen, panniers bulging. They owned a car—it would have been very hard to live and parent in Arkansas without one, even in this college town; they didn't know anyone who did—but maintained this vestige of alternative cred, biking to campus and stores. (Were there college towns in other countries? It seemed so American, for a commercial and residential ecosystem to grow up around a university planted hundreds of miles from nowhere. Growing up in Alberta, P'd never heard of such a thing.)

He pulled out avocados, chèvre, smoked salmon, two bottles of wine, no doubt excellent. P unplugged the Crock-Pot when his back was turned. The soup only had an hour left; she could refrigerate and resurrect. She had waited, though, until she could be sure that the promised alternative would materialize.

He uncorked and decanted, swirled olive oil into a pan, smashed garlic, every gesture large and noisy, biceps flexing, glasses slipping down his nose, as she sat and watched and waited for a chance to mention what had happened with Aakash. When the pans were sizzling and redolent, he served her a glass of wine with a flourish. She did an awkward curtsy thing on her barstool. She welcomed the drink but also wondered if she would shortly hear that accusing voice that alcohol had lately brought on, wondered if in fact she wanted the drink because she wanted to hear it.

She sipped to quell her nervousness about drinking, no, her nervousness about talking to him about the kid. "I think Aakash had his computer upstairs when I got home," she said, sotto voce.

"What?" he said, whisking fast and hard.

She repeated and he looked at her like, *What the hell?* "Did you check his room?" She hadn't. He cocked his head like, *What the hell, stupid?* which was kind of what she was thinking herself now. "Stir this." He ran up the stairs and then walked down a few minutes later.

"No luck?" She took another sip. That thing was happening in her head, but Deepa walked in just then and interrupted.

"Light of our lives!" Mac crowed. He was particularly proud of that nickname and the way it reminded Deepa of what her name meant. *In Sanskrit and Tamil,* he would say.

He said it, went the voice in P's head, *to people who didn't know the difference any more than he did.* Yep.

"Dad's cooking?" Deepa asked P. "Should I have a snack?"

"Ha ha." Mac pointed a spatula at her. "It'll be ready in fifteen. Set the table."

"I have homework," she said.

"What have you been doing all afternoon?"

"I go to Maisie's after school on Thursdays," she said, like, *duh.*

"What's stopping you from doing homework at Maisie's?" he asked, arranging salads with quick flicks of his wrist.

"Mom?" she asked.

P got up and steered her into the dining room by her shoulders. "Clear the table." She went over and studied Aakash, who in turn was riveted by his iPad. "Help your sister," she told him, repeating it when he was slow, then finding excuses to tidy the living room herself. "Where's your computer?" she asked, but he appeared not to hear, going through to the kitchen. By the time she followed him there, she saw him disappearing upstairs and when he came down with a laundry basket, P tapped Mac on the arm. He looked at her. *What?* She indicated Aakash, already walking past them swiftly and without eye contact.

"Hand that over," Mac said to him.

"What, I, *what?*"

"You think we don't know?" Mac pulled the laptop from within the laundry and opened it on the island. A couple of healthy-looking young women scissored on a king-size bed while all around them thumbnails advertised other options. Deepa came in from the kitchen to get forks and Aakash slammed the laptop shut while P ushered her daughter back into the dining room and Mac berated their son: "Have we taught you nothing? Why do you think you're not allowed to have your computer upstairs? That industry is irredeemably, institutionally exploitative of women. It will warp how you view them, gradually and permanently. It is warping girls your age, who think they have to perform to standards set by professional sex workers. Not okay!"

Aakash appeared to be hyperventilating, his hands over his face. "I know, I know. I'm sorry. *I know.*"

P wanted to hold him, rub his back, tell him *breathe*, tell him it was okay. Except it wasn't: Mac said she let the kids walk all over her, said she undermined him when he disciplined them, and by all objective measures, what Aakash had done was wrong, so why did she feel so terrible for him? She couldn't bear to see him suffer for what was surely a natural urge. And he hadn't been viewing anything twisted: capably athletic, full-grown women having a good time with each other, so what? Okay, pretending to have a good time, and waxed and airbrushed, all of that, but at least he hadn't been watching anything, say, obviously coercive. Voyeurism: not good, but understandable at his age.

"You are so naive," Mac marveled, when she asked him about this later. The night had been a huge frigging mess: Aakash had run straight back up to bed; P explained what was going on to Deepa; the three of them had eaten in silence.

After cleaning the kitchen with Deepa—house rule, the cook didn't clean (though on P's cooking nights, which is to say, most nights, she did a quick pre-dinner clean and brief post-cleaning clean—things just ran better that way)—P went up and tried to talk to Aakash, but he wouldn't take his face out of his pillow. When she asked Mac if he could talk to the boy, he said, "He disobeyed us. Apart from harming women, he's harming himself. How's he going to ever develop a healthy relationship if all his ideas on sex come from porn? We've been over this: you don't do him any favors by being lenient."

She knew all that. "I know all that. I just, I didn't think he should be shamed for it, especially in front of his sister."

"She needs to know that her parents—well, her father, anyway—are willing to stand up for women."

You wouldn't have even noticed if it weren't for me, that voice inside her head retorted, unfairly: he was cooking dinner. *You weren't even paying attention.* But they were partners, and it was a father's job to talk to a son about these things. Somehow, though, she couldn't get past the sense, wrong as it was, that it was sad to stomp on what looked like curiosity and human desire. And some women liked porn, didn't they?

"Maggie Nelson says in *The Argonauts* that she likes porn," she told Mac, who appeared to be formatting his CV in bed.

"You've got to be kidding me right now." He cast a skeptical glance up over his screen at her. "What is she, some second-wave TERF?"

"Hardly—she's married to a trans man."

"Oh, I'm sure they're fine with trans men. It's trans women they refuse to recognize."

How did they get so far off topic? "Are you going to talk to Aakash?"

"Let him think a while on what he did. I mean, there should be some penalty, but we can figure that out tomorrow."

That wasn't what she meant. She still had questions. How long had this been going on? How did he get access? Was it only recorded porn? What if he'd been exposed himself? They had to talk to him. They had to get him to talk. How? Maybe she should find a counselor? But: now?

That was the pandemic's first night in their household. The

next day, they decided to keep the kids, both of whom had suffered childhood asthma, home from school. That weekend, schools were shuttered.

Now they were home together full-time.

Which wasn't the worst thing in the world.

The children were reasonably academically motivated, though P found herself working with them to make sure they knew what they were supposed to be doing at various points in the day. It was sweet, spending days in their ambit, checking in, helping a little. One afternoon, all three of them worked together on the sofa, P in the middle, Deepa leaning on her shoulder and interfering with her typing.

She and Mac decided it was appropriate to deprive Aakash of his personal computer for a week. He put up no fight. He didn't seem to want to go anywhere near it, instead starting back in on a series of novels he'd loved when he was twelve, regressing into older pleasures, old comforts. The hardest thing, P imagined, was knowing his sister knew. Deepa didn't ask her or Mac any questions about it, not at all. It seemed both kids just wanted the whole episode to sink away. Unless they talked with each other? It seemed unlikely, but Deepa had a way with him. They bickered when they were with their parents, but she had caught them exchanging smirks, come upon them in tears from laughing at something on one of their phones. Mac would ask to see the screen, but P never did: adults could never see what was funny in memes; it just killed the mood. Someone in the house needed to be laughing the way they laughed.

Those first weeks, though, no one laughed much as the pandemic wrapped itself around the globe like a thousand rubber bands, like the globe was made of rubber bands, rubber bands all the way down.

ə❧

Freud's *The Uncanny*—essay beloved of translators. The opening section is nothing but a discussion of the titular word: in German, *das unheimlich*. Its root, *heimlich*, means familiar or belonging to the home but also secret or hidden. It is a word, says Freud, *whose meaning develops toward an ambivalence, until it finally coincides with its opposite, unheimlich,* just as Freud ran into the wandering Jew of his own self, re-entering his very own compartment. Unheimlich names a condition where what is most familiar is also what's most threatening, *that class of the terrifying which leads back to something long known to us, once very familiar.* Examples include severed body parts, mirrors, shadows.

Incest, though he doesn't mention that—the uncanny is the home playing field of the gothic.

(And a chunk of food gone down the wrong pipe? That works: *Heimlich* the maneuver is invoked when what has entered the body and was meant to sustain it will instead destroy it if not expelled. Heimlich becomes unheimlich when eating becomes choking.)

Freud proves his case by quoting a dictionary assembled by the elder Brother Grimm. Who would know the uncanny any better? A stepmother is an uncanny mother, for example: a figure resembling a mother who, taking up residence in the home, turns maternal care into a lethal act.

ə❧

When Dr. Stein published his article on the Rob de Laffecteur, it had only been off the market for a few years.

Was the rob altogether a fraud? asks Dr. Stein. *Was it a big lie with a little truth? Does the secrecy which surrounds it wholly damn it?*

A new idea had taken hold: inducing malaria. After the fever sweated out the syphilis, the malaria would be cured with quinine (relative of chloroquine, now being groundlessly touted by our president as a remedy for our latest plague).

In science we are fully justified in not accepting a conclusion until the grounds upon which that conclusion is based are laid before us, Dr. Stein concludes, crediting Gustav von Bunge, the physiologist, for this line.

Is he quoting von Bunge, though? The only other place I find this quote is an article published in July 1913, a month after Stein's, in the *Journal of the American Institute of Homeopathy.* Neither article cites a source.

And while Boyveau-Laffecteur apparently said *Every secret remedy performs miracles because it is secret; disclose the secret, it becomes inert,* he had more than one product with exactly the same secret, so it's pretty obvious how a disclosure would affect it. Otherwise, this statement seems as dubious as the von Bunge one is self-evident. Also, I have uncovered no evidence for the existence of the plant bécatunga.

వ

Napoleon was truly a man of his time and his interest in the Rob de Laffecteur implies that he, like every other man of his time, suffered the French affliction. Was that what killed him?

He died at fifty-two in exile on Saint Helena, after gaining weight and suffering gastric symptoms. His personal physician performed the autopsy and declared the cause of death: an ulcerated cancerous lesion in the stomach.

But in 1961, someone analyzing the emperor's hair discovered it to have elevated arsenic levels. Had he in fact been poisoned? If so, by whom? It would have to have been someone sequestered with him, off on that extraordinarily remote Atlantic island.

Eventually suspicion landed very near, indeed—a locked-room mystery. Subject to the afflictions of his time, was he killed by the predilections of his time?

A fashion had arisen in eighteenth century decorating for certain greens—cupric arsenite, in particular, or Scheele's Green, *characterized variously as apple green and light sea green,* says Patrick Baty in *The Anatomy of Color.* These pigments were fixed with arsenic.

Napoleon's home in Saint Helena was appropriately decorated for the royal exile, who was famously fond of green. His bathroom in particular is often mentioned: a small room in which he would attempt to relieve his tummy troubles by soaking in a deep copper tub. The steam in this close little room, together with the humid climate of his unchosen home, released arsenical fumes from his stylish wallpapers. Could these have killed him?

It's tempting to think so, but in fact, this most uncanny of diagnoses—literally killed by his home—has been debunked. *Advances in Anatomic Pathology* published an article in 2011, "The Medical Mystery of Napoleon Bonaparte: An Interdisciplinary Exposé," which decisively concluded: *Before long the once powerful Emperor would succumb not to battle wounds inflicted by gallant rivals or to the toxic schemes of vile adversaries, but to gastric cancer, an enemy that still remains unconquered two centuries later.*

ॐ

As I have said, the French- and English-language sides of the Great Chartreuse's website are not identical. For instance, the French side relates this little anecdote, omitted in the English flipside: *In 1611,*

Cardinal Richelieu warmly thanked the Reverend Father of the Paris Charterhouse, who had sent him a bezoar to cure an 'unfortunate illness.'

Bezoar: from the French *bezoard*, which originates in a Persian word for antidote. It would not be out of place in Galland's *Arabian Nights.*

"Bezoar" is also the name of a story by the Mexican writer Guadalupe Nettel. (Its translator, Rahul Bery, is a member of the small South Asians Translating European Languages Club to which I belong in my imagination. In my imagination, we meet monthly, sitting in plush high-backed chairs, Bombay Sapphire gin and tonics sweating on carved-elephant side tables, exchanging laughs, gossip, repartee, resting our feet on a brocaded ottoman.)

Nettel's story opens with a quote from Ambroise Paré, that famous debunker of panaceas: *Another supposed cure-all was the bezoar stone. These stones are secretions found in the stomachs of animals that devour their own hair, especially in a certain Indian goat, and it is said that they prevent melancholy and jaundice and that they serve as an antidote against all kinds of poisoning.*

Bezoar stone: protection against mental illness, turning yellow, or being poisoned, within your home or otherwise.

ه‌ب

Poison: a term used as much as a metaphor as literally. Alcohol poisoning: too much of a good thing. Poisoning one's mind: an uncanny process.

ه‌ب

Also, by the way, arsenic is an anti-syphilitic. It's almost as though Napoleon was trying to auto-suffumigate. If we want to give him that kind of credit.

❦

The kids did school virtually.

She and Mac taught virtually.

P and her students dissected language, literary structure, Quebec, Mauritius, Senegal, scalpeling out thin sheets of meaning and holding them to the light. Nothing to do with super-spreaders or droplets or to mask or not to mask (except for once in a while when a book presciently referred to contagion). The work lifted her spirits. She thought it was the same for her students—they clung to her through the screen.

Mac canceled his first few classes. (Why? Did he think it would all go away if he waited it out? When she asked, he just shook his head.) When he resumed teaching, he shortened his classes, always letting out early. He had been a wildly popular if divisive teacher but didn't feel the same magic online.

"I just think they have enough to worry about without worrying about their classes," he said, frowning disapproval as she emerged, dazed, from three hours discussing Leila Slimani's *Chanson Douce/The Perfect Nanny* over Cadabra, the video-conferencing platform and maybe spyware that none of them had heard of before but that was now becoming everyone's front door to social or professional life.

Was she burning her students out? They seemed to be enjoying class, but you just never knew. It was exhausting but she felt it was equally sustaining: they were still connecting with each other by wrangling over books. The core of their enterprise was untouched. Maybe she needed that reassurance.

Meanwhile, Mac was consumed with two new consulting gigs: one on provision of equipment for home offices—should companies pay for it? The calculus was shifting rapidly now that everyone was working from home. And the other on a guide to online meeting etiquette and microaggressions. He did real work in and for the real world, improving people's lives, while she paddled around in her little literary pond, teaching novels and writing her secret essay on her favorite color—could anything be more selfish? She couldn't bear the selfishness sometimes, one reason translation was easier to commit to: as pleasurable as it was, it was in the service of some other writer, opening the gate to the global market—English!—for an author who might not otherwise have access. And translators virtually never got recognition outside their own circles. Although this was changing, few expected it would change much anytime soon, and neither P's chagrin at her lack of credit nor the concomitant virtue she accrued were likely to be affected.

In that way, Mac was maybe in a similar position. If those reports and guides he wrote had authorship, he would be a co-author. He did research; he wrote. It just wasn't scholarly as such. It was applied, not arid. It had immediate, real-world value, unlike literature and, let's be honest, much scholarship. That in itself should count for something.

Amid all this, she felt they couldn't simply let Aakash drop. P did a little research, she got a book on boys and sex by a feminist writer, very informative. It seemed to her that Mac, well, it wasn't that he was wrong, exactly, but the main thing, it seemed to her, and to Peggy Orenstein, the writer of this book, was to keep the conversation going, just what didn't seem to be happening. But Mac was Aakash's father, a man, smart and dependable and not exactly out of touch with the world. If anything, P was more out of touch. They just saw things so differently.

"We do talk," Mac said, when she tried to ask him.

"About porn?"

"We've told the kids about the dangers of porn," he said.

"We've warned them off it, but . . ." It felt to her that they needed to say something positive, about sexuality. Guide them.

"Kids don't learn about sex from their parents," he explained, which seemed inarguable. "We just need to keep them safe and healthy."

Now she quoted to Mac from the book on boys and sex, hoping to get him to read it, but she could never seem to find a tidbit that enticed him instead of apparently confirming what he already knew. He was glad she was learning so much about boys and men, but he didn't need to read it. "I live it," he said. Plus it intersected so heavily with his areas of study.

Once more, it seemed there was nothing to talk about or nothing that talking would solve.

She managed to confirm with Aakash that he had not exposed his body. "Did you see anything violent? Or with children?" she asked, bringing up the topic awkwardly one day when she went up to say good night to him, after reading in the book for courage.

"No, Mom. Geez," he said, "come on," as though taking his father's side: they had this under control.

Good, good boy. His sheet was pulled up across his bare chest, his jaw hard in the light from his lamp. She patted his knee tentatively, and took herself away, her face burning to recall a different dream she had, around the beginning of the year, the strangest of dreams kicking off the strangest of years, not just for her: for practically every human on the planet.

৵

Once a year or so, P's subconscious shocked her by conjuring an erotic dream about a wholly unlikely object: a student she'd never consciously thought attractive, or the ice-queen girlfriend of the boy she'd loved in university, decades earlier. Her dreams had always been vivid, but in her first year of living with Mac, the first person with whom she'd consistently shared a bed, she woke frequently at night—the main and indeed perhaps only way that people remember their dreams—and her dreams became as vivid as reality. She would dream he had done something that angered her and stay as mad in waking life as if he really had done it. He teased her about it in a way that made it seem as if, otherwise, he took her anger seriously. After that period of adjustment, though, sharing a bed became normal and the dreams drifted back into their own world, even as she started keeping better records of them.

She had kept a journal since her teens, but when the children came along she switched from writing it at night to writing in the morning. It made it easier to record her dreams, though that wasn't why she switched. She switched because evening was the rare interval she and Mac had together alone. Also because her attention had turned inward: off the street, into the home. Away from the energy of New York City, its swishing streets and pro- verbial grit and the mashedupness of everyone and everything— she'd fallen so hard for it when they arrived, so different even from Montreal: even that most uninhibited of Canadian cities seemed gentle and whimsical by contrast, utterly Canadian in its failure ever fully to take a stand. It was part of what attracted her to Mac, early on: the unapologetic brashness of Americans, their willingness to commit to their opinions without apology, so refreshing. It made the Canadian national pastimes of hedging and apologizing feel exhausting by contrast, and also like a luxury. It was why she agreed on a postdoc at NYU instead of the Sorbonne, apart from the impossible question of what Mac would do in France. They had hoped for something for him at Sciences Po, but without French it was hard to contemplate. New York had something for both of them.

But after the postdocs, they swung onto the carousel of freelancing and adjunct teaching that let people like them keep a Brooklyn apartment half a block from a shuffleboard local or super-authentic dive bar, enjoying shouty Sunday brunches in steamy diners, Saturday picnics after the farmers market in Fort Greene. The road forked with kids. P wanted a steadier existence, and she had a green card now, which made her fully employable on both sides of the border. And it wasn't as though Mac's US citizenship would work against him if he got a job offer north of the forty-ninth. When they went on the job market, though, their destiny turned out to be Arkansas, of all places, where she got an offer.

In retrospect, it was amazing that she got him to move here for her. But maybe he was attracted by the possibilities of the business school, endowed by and named for the entrepreneur who had turned this isolated if scenic pocket of the country into an economic powerhouse. Indeed, within two years Mac managed to leverage adjuncting into a visiting professorship and, from there, hit the tenure track running. So what had happened?

In her analysis, Mac wasn't suited to academic life in so relatively staid an institution. He needed a position to be created for him, some kind of Chair in Innovation that let him do his thing. High-powered private universities like Princeton or Duke had faculty whose main work was public engagement, though sometimes land-grant universities randomly got endowments for that kind of thing. With all the money in northwest Arkansas, and the brainpower it sucked in, it seemed a likely place, but when she Googled "innovation UArk," having thought she heard mentions of the term and sensing that Mac was—unlike her—at odds with his context, anything she encountered seemed like a mask. There was something on the education side, but it seemed to be about shoring up public institutions, "meeting twenty-first century demands," and so on, making education more practical and goal-oriented. On the business side, it was about, well, business. There was an office for entrepreneurship and innovation, with a slick, appealing website that offered courses called things like "The Heart of the Customer," offering the chance to "Explore why empathy is a catalyst for innovation." It was in such meetings, she suspected, that the sausage of monetizing human emotions got made: where a Nike marketing person would say, maybe in sign language so as to have plausible deniability, *Hey—a marriage equality ad campaign! Gay people have money and they'll overlook our factories full of little Pakistani eight-year-olds if our magazine ads are stamped with the Human Rights Campaign logo.*

Mac didn't propose ways for companies to capitalize on social change, he pointed out changes to make companies better suited to women, which helped recruiting and retention, which did make those companies more successful . . . was that the same thing? She often felt, in conversations with Mac, that she was merely naive, that her social analysis was stuck in late-eighties resistance to neo-liberalism. He'd had to keep up; he worked *with* corporations but wasn't *of* them; he was fluent in corporate lingo and activist lingo, but he didn't code-switch, he meshed.

On the descent from her son's room, though, what in fact was P thinking about? Was she thinking about Mac's CV and how it would demonstrate that he was or wasn't qualified for tenure? Or was she thinking about a shocking, shameful dream, a version of which would repeat a few months later? Was it either-or? Think of her mind, on the descent, as traveling both of those high-walled trenches simultaneously, her mind splitting along two parallel tracks, anxiety and insecurity, dug by self-doubt. Think of those trenches as starting to burrow into the undermind, where it will turn out that they are not parallel but bend together in long arcs, in the undermind where, traveling long arcs, they meet.

ৡ

The Uncanny makes a brief reference to a monograph by Otto Rank, Freud's former student, *The Double*, a study of the unending human fascination with replicant selves. Rank says that *primitive cultures* and *ancient civilizations* have in common a belief in *the human soul as being an exact copy of the body.* (NB: this doesn't jive with anything I know about the Hindu treatment of the soul, which is plastic, evolving through lives and bodies, not fundamentally humanoid. Nor do I know whether Rank would classify my natal culture as "primitive" or as an "ancient civilization.")

But where do our doubles live on earth? In our shadows, in reflections on water or in glass, and in the alter egos—our other selves—who untether themselves from us in dreams to live out alternative realities, no more subject to our volition than is our waking life.

ৡ

Guadalupe Nettel's "Bezoar" is written as the journal of a woman in a rehab clinic, who, at the request of her psychologist, writes the history of her addictions. Most are banal: cigarettes, alcohol, pot, etc., each supplanting the one previous. But the first, and the only one that has endured, is pulling out strands of her hair one at a time.

Plucking out her hair, from the age of nine, gave her *an indescribable sense of relief.* The root of the strand, though, *provoked an animal aversion in me. It wasn't disgust—more like a kind of hatred, along with the need to eliminate it as soon as possible. The first thing that occurred to me was to put the bulb in my mouth and swallow it; maybe this was because it came from inside my body, and so it only seemed natural to return it to the bottomless depths it had come from.*

I have never pulled out my hair but understand the compulsion; I pull at cuticle shreds, seeking the pain and relief. Oh, the shameful evidence of the disappeared tranche, the pink underlayers exposed, vulnerable to heat or acid, to dishwashing or lemon-squeezing.

Often, I pull off the cuticle with my teeth, and swallow.

Otto Rank doesn't start with anthropology. He starts with literature: E. T. A. Hoffmann, Hans Christian Andersen, Edgar Allan Poe, Dostoevsky. Over and over characters are pursued by their shadows, confront their reflections in water or glass, find men identical to them sitting at their desks, courting their women, sneering at them malignantly. The doubles are rivals, in other words, and in virtually all of Rank's examples there's a showdown between them. *The impulse to rid oneself of the uncanny opponent in a violent manner belongs to the essential features of the motif.* This town ain't big enough for the both of us. (José Saramago's *The Double,* written nearly a century later, still fulfills this formula.)

Freud notes this helical shift: if the soul was the first double, then *the double, from having been an assurance of immortality, becomes a harbinger of death.*

Neither Freud nor Rank treats an example where the doubles *are* women, neither speculates on how this might shift the fatal equation.

❧

Now, P's morning ritual of journal writing was morphing, becoming notes toward her strange personal essay, a piece that had begun as something delectable but was starting to disturb her a little.

She had started writing in a journal at nineteen, during her early struggle with depression—that is to say, after she succumbed to her depression and received an intervention, by means of which she arrived at the will to live. Until she was pulled under, she had never thought of life as a task voluntarily undertaken. Chosen, it seemed more precious. Anyway, the journal was prescribed by a therapist but P found she unexpectedly enjoyed it, not only the process of selecting what from the day was interesting enough to set down in ink, not only the feeling of the pen running over the page making lines and shapes in color, but also reading over it later in moments of doubt: when her mother reinvented their shared past or a boyfriend later denied having said what he'd previously said more than once, she could go back and confirm she was right. It was a private satisfaction. And also, flipping back through the pages, she found herself entertained: her life had been interesting, at least to her, at least condensed into moments worth recording.

And layered thick in the journal were the dreams. Often they were quite obvious: for the eight months in her twenties when she'd worked in admin for the National Film Board, she dreamed of switchboards and to-do lists. When her first translation was accepted for publication, a dream took her to a garden party where the novel's characters drank champagne. They toasted her drily, ironically, almost reluctantly, without getting up. She thought she made out the author at the far end of the lawn, talking anima-tedly with a woman. He never looked at her.

૨૭

I cannot substantiate John Bethune Stein's quotes but I do find online a couple of references to the doctor himself:

He was a member of the Metropolitan Museum of Art, at the cheapest level of membership.

He was, further, the translator of a book called *Syphilis and Similar Diseases of the Mouth*.

But *Diseases of the Mouth for Physicians, Dentists, Medical and Dental Students, by Prof. Dr. F. Zinsser, Translated and Edited by John Bethune Stein, M.D.* is now the name of a piece of art on the home-page of Grant Czuj, an artist who graduated from Detroit's College of Creative Studies in spring 2020, and then, that fall, matriculated at Yale School of Art. In his graduation photo, he wears an N95 mask.

In 2005, when Czuj was seventeen years old, he was sentenced to jail for drunk-driving a speedboat into a couple of pontoon boats whose occupants were injured and killed. He served almost ten years.

૨૭

What does any of this have to do with chartreuse? I set out to write about a color I love and instead have been led down these garden paths.

No. Wrong idiom. To be led down (or up) the garden path is to be deceived. I am not deceived. I have taken forking paths toward places unknown.

A garden path sentence is one that, while grammatically correct, initially misleads readers and ultimately confuses them, so they need to go back over the line to understand what it actually means: The horse raced past the barn fell. We painted the wall with cracks.

Am *I* leading readers up the garden path? Am I, too, being led?

ॐ

I remember a book about myths and legends, says Nettel's narrator, speaking of her childhood. *In it there was a drawing of a woman with hair all the way down to her waist; she carried a marvellous gem in one hand. According to the author, in a place very far away from our continent there existed a stone or hairball with healing powers. The bezoar was the remedy for all poisons, a stone of perfect calm. This discovery troubled me. On one hand, it seemed difficult for me to believe that a gem could be confused with a hairball. On the other, there was something oddly coherent to the legend: if I pulled out a hair, it was for that sensation of perfect tranquility and calm, even if it only lasted a fraction of a second.*

In my recollection, "Bezoar" ended with the narrator throwing herself from her third-story window, which *gives on to the edge of the cliff,* over the ocean.

I had copied into my journal her thoughts on receiving a letter from her lover: *I was torn between throwing myself out the window right then and there or waiting until the lights of the clinic went off, so that the last thing I saw would be the lighthouse shining over the bay.*

But in fact the story ends with the narrator saying she is meeting her lover, that day, at the cliff, and that only one of them will return. They are driving each other batty with their compulsions (his as minor as hers: cracking his knuckles). One of them has to go.

Nowhere in the story does it mention what floor her room is on.

ॐ

It seems to me that once you decide to find doubles, you find them every-where, Michelle Kuo writes in *Reading with Patrick,* her account of her friendship with a young incarcerated man in Arkansas. *How does a single human mind come to be divided into two beings, into a life that "does not become" and a life that does?*

I, too, have a friendship with a young incarcerated man. Kuo's friend was once her student. My friend read an essay I wrote in an anthology that circulated through the jails, and sent me a postcard. I live in Arkansas; my friend is in Arizona.

Writ large, his story, as with Kuo's friend's, is one that repeats ad nauseam in this country: a young man makes a young man's mistake and because the social membrane that should protect him is tissue-thin and ragged (mostly because of circumstances attributable to race), he is chuted away from the remainder of his own youth into a locked room.

Writ small, it's this: a single human mind and the multiple biographical possibilities it contains.

My friend in Arizona was sentenced to eleven-and-a-quarter years for trafficking in stolen goods. His version is that he bought a cello after seeing someone play one in a punk band. He was a musician but didn't know how hard it is to play a cello. So he tried to sell it to a music store he frequented. Turned out it was stolen.

The pandemic in prisons is its own story: what it is to be subject to a higher authority on whether you are allowed to or made to wear a mask, on whether and for how long you will share a cell with a sick person, on whether and when you will receive treatment.

My friend in Arizona told me the first time a man he knew (an old man, a friend) was carried out on a stretcher with COVID-19. That man died.

My friend in Arizona told me he was paranoid about germs, had stopped socializing, was sterilizing everything he touched.

My friend in Arizona told me his mother had gotten COVID. Thankfully, she didn't die.

My friend in Arizona stopped calling for a few weeks. He had gotten COVID.

My friend in Arizona was randomly shuffled to a new cellblock, a new cell.

My friend in Arizona tells me he'll not be able to call for a bit because—owing to a COVID-19 outbreak—they're not being allowed out in the yard. His information streams are limited but even he knows how hard it is to catch COVID-19 outdoors.

The Marshall Project tells us one in five prisoners has had COVID-19, four times the rate of infection in the general population.

In America, the search for a cure for syphilis is inextricably bound with experimentation on people of color and internees, American doctors infecting Black sharecroppers at the Tuskegee Institute, American doctors infecting prisoners and mental patients in Guatemala. Why do we say "evil stepmother" but have no catch phrase for the uncanny doctor, who kills, who harms, or for a state that victimizes the citizens whose welfare is its primarily responsibility?

One feature of the usual script for plague: the disease invariably comes from somewhere else, said Susan Sontag in *AIDS and Its Metaphors,*

listing fifteenth-century names for syphilis. The English called it the "French pox," while it was *morbus Germanicus to the Parisians, the Naples sickness to the Florentines, the Chinese disease to the Japanese.* We want to believe that plagues visit or are visited upon us from afar, that they are not our own, much less our own fault.

So COVID-19 was the Chinese flu to our president and our nation's first response was to shut its doors to more dang foreigners, but was that new? No, it was habitual. He campaigned on putting his shoulder against our doors to the south, and one of his first actions was an executive order slamming doors on seven Muslim nations, xenophobia as policy.

In summer 2020, during the BLM uprisings, many Black folks got notes from white people they'd not heard from in ages, asking how they were. Now it's spring 2021, the pandemic loosening its grip, vaccinations bringing optimism, and I got a note from a Black colleague, asking how I'm doing. *Uh-oh,* I thought, *there's been anti-Asian hate crime,* and checked the headlines: yes, a Filipino-Chinese woman beaten up in NYC.

Not someone I would have thought I had anything in common with, but then the only other Asian in my neighborhood is Filipino-Chinese, and, as I said earlier, when the white lady across the street sees her out walking, she calls her by my name.

ॐ

In the first months of the pandemic, when everyone was hearing from old exes, P had dreams of tearful, joyful reunions with two old friends: one who had, years earlier, simply stopped returning her emails; and another who had, more recently, violently broken with her. Apparently, P had failed to proffer unconditional love? She hadn't realized until he erupted in fury and long-suppressed discontent. She dreamed of him twice, just before and just after his birthday. She dreamed her mother died suddenly and without warning. She dreamed of dancing with her sister, who had not phoned, not once, during the pandemic. P had emailed, asking after her and her husband, and her sister wrote back saying they were fine, thanks. In the dream, she and her sister wore bathrobes, their hair was damp and they were young.

Awakened at 3:30 from the last in a series of short dreams, like short films, not unenjoyable and yet clearly all driven by COVID, P wrote in her journal. The final one was of a car coming toward me: a formerly green sports car, now rusted to cloudy patches. I am on a country road, a hill rising sharply from the road's shoulder to my right, a farmhouse and fields to my left. The car approaches, swerves, corrects, so I know there's a problem but it's not until it nears that I really understand it: the woman is drunk and panicked and is aiming for me, I think because she has somehow decided this will keep her steady. I decide my best strategy—after waving my arms and shaking my head 'no' at her—is to lure her toward the house and then jump out of the way at the last minute. But apparently that decision was distressful enough to wake me up.

And twice, nine months apart, she dreamed of having sex with her son. Was there such a thing as a Jocasta complex? It seemed appropriate: she had always thought that Freud was wrong when he called the Oedipus complex the subconscious desire to sleep with the mother and kill the father, because it only became a complex when the fait accompli was revealed, to the perpetrator and to the public. Oedipus never *desired* that. He killed some random dude at a crossroads; he married a widowed queen. It made sense for Freud to call it a complex to the extent that such desires are often suppressed, that we can't admit them and so don't need to acknowledge them until they wreak their terrible havoc, but was that what was happening now? She had no conscious desire for her son and the dreams weren't really erotic. She didn't awaken aroused; she awoke disturbed and disgusted. But in the dream, the sex was just somehow part of the maternal equation. He didn't have condoms and she chastised him just like a mother would. He rooted for her breast as he had when he was a baby.

She recalled reading a *New Yorker* article that described a mother and son under attack by Haitian rebels, a scene from a collection of short stories largely set in Haiti. The son is fourteen, and the crazy-eyed soldiers force the mother to give him oral sex, as though wanting to do the thing that would be most damaging to the child, the thing that would ream his psyche, make him want to blind himself and rampage, destroy the world that made him. The mother, on her knees, reassures him. "It's okay, because we love each other." If they don't do what the soldiers say, they will be killed, tortured, raped. It is her job to take the thing that will otherwise destroy her child, and neutralize it with love.

In P's dream, it was like that. Unless that was just what she needed to believe.

She had read somewhere about the common desire to have known the lover as a child. She found it puzzling: What was at its root? A desire to possess the lover whole? A desire to see the future: to see in the child the lover had been the child they might have together? Mac's reaction, on seeing pictures of her when she was small, had touched her: "So cute," he'd said. "I wish I'd known you then."

Now, though, she thought about how it startled her sometimes to see their son shirtless: he was a basketball player, just the sort of boy she might have crushed on at his age. She didn't wish to have known Mac when he was small, but wondered if they might have gravitated to each other as teens. Was it natural to be unsettled by seeing your child become the age you yourself were when you first articulated desire? Especially given your child was made in the image of a person you once were headily attracted to? It seemed akin to a crush on a cousin, an experience she had at sixteen— common, she learned from the internet. She felt attraction for her father when she was fourteen—normal, she learned from a book. This, now, without doubt, was the worst of those attractions, but she also had no conscious experience of it, only a subconscious one, which in some ways felt more real: perhaps she was lying to herself, but the subconscious didn't lie. She tried to do research but apparently the idea was so shameful that no one out there would admit to it. She was alone. Then again, who wasn't these days? She would have to learn to live with it.

ॐ

Our nature lies in movement; complete calm is death. —Pascal, *Pensées*, copied into Bruce Chatwin's notebook and quoted in *The Songlines*, his quasi-comic treatise on the human urge to go, go, go.

When everyone else was rereading *The Decameron* and *The Plague*, this is where I turned in confinement. *A study of the Great Malady: horror of home.* —Baudelaire, *Journaux Intimes*.

ॐ

In August 2020, an article proposed that COVID is spreading fastest in the economic powerhouses of the developing world, where populations are most mobile: India and Brazil.

Is pandemic, then, endemic in human nature, in human progress?

Are we meant to stay in place—isolated within a language, mindset, gene pool; loyal to home, close to family—or are we meant to move and mix?

Now, in spring 2021, the United States leads the world in rate of infection. We are first in the world, in so many things, but are we first world? It doesn't feel that way from within: blatantly corrupt, rampantly hierarchical, with large swathes of our population falling through the cracks.

What a perfect idiom! Nations are not land masses to be defended and exploited; they are ideas, most solid as metaphors. So the image of this nation cracking along all its fault lines, broken apart by its faults, as the vulnerable—the old, the obese, the opioid addicts and meth users, the imprisoned and undocumented—tumble off its parting edges into the void, is as terribly right as it is terribly wrong.

My point is that illness is not a metaphor, Susan Sontag says in *Illness as Metaphor,* before describing all the ways it is used as metaphor and some of the ways she objects.

But everything used as metaphor has literal existence as well. That is the power of the metaphor: it harnesses one side of something real to turn the beacon of its descriptive powers onto something else.

Color, however, can only properly be described in terms of something else. Does that make it intrinsically metaphoric?

Wittgenstein: *When we're asked "What do the words 'red', 'blue', 'black', 'white' mean?" we can, of course, immediately point to things which have these colours, but our ability to explain the meanings of these words goes no further!*

When someone mentions a color, I have no idea what they are seeing. What does anyone else see, when they see blue or red or chartreuse? How does the sky in fact look to them? We can never perceive in common, only make linguistic-perceptual agreements. As, I suppose, with any other sense-experience. I know that pain is unpleasant and the pie I made last night was agreeable to everyone who ate it, but what exactly is sweet or sharp to them? I don't know.

This troubled Wittgenstein. *When blind people speak, as they like to do, of blue sky and other specifically visual phenomena, the sighted person often says "Who knows what he imagines that to mean?"—But why doesn't he say this about other sighted people? It is of course a wrong expression to begin with. That which I am writing about so tediously, may be obvious to someone whose mind is less decrepit . . . The rule-governed nature of our languages permeates our life.*

But when he asked, *When would we say of someone, he doesn't have our concept of pain?* I thought, *Studies show that we say it when we are a white doctor and the person we are speaking of is Black.*

à❧

Color, felt Delacroix, has a more mysterious and powerful influence on us than anything else—"It acts, we might say," he writes, "without our knowledge." —ALEXANDER THEROUX, *The Secondary Colors*

à❧

I looked again at William Ranken's *The Amateur Boxer*, and didn't see it as chartreuse any longer but as mustard. I deleted it from my essay. I looked the next day and it was green once more and I restored it to my essay. *Green*, says Alexander Theroux, is *the color of more force and guises than are countable . . . at once the preternaturally ambiguous color*

of life and death, the vernal sign of vitality, and the livid tinge of corrup-
tion, a "dialectical lyric" (to borrow a term from Kierkegaard), respond-
ing with the kind of answers that perhaps depend less on itself than on the
questions we ask of it.

But my daughter and I also had this experience: we watched *The Flying Lovers of Vitebsk*, a small lovely play about Marc and Bella Chagall, beamed to us from the Bristol Old Vic. I mirrored my laptop to the TV. The play's backdrop was composed of silk panels lit by gorgeous washes of color, such that all the panels would be variations on a shade, each panel consistent within itself but each varying slightly from the other. But there was also this variation, which my daughter pointed out: *Look,* she said, *it's blue on the TV and green on your computer.* Which was it? There was no way to know. Without seeing it in person, there was no way to know, but even sitting side by side in the theater, all we would know was that we were seeing the same color, even while we would have no idea whether we were seeing the same color.

ॐ

My study is on the third story.

It is painted in two shades of chartreuse. When the first, lighter, coat was applied to the walls and the low, acutely peaked ceiling, it looked yellow. *Man, that yellow is intense,* said the painter as he descended the steep stairs. I despaired. What had I done? I hate yellow.

(I even hate the word *yellow*—look at the shape of it! Contrast: the ugly opening consonant—I don't disapprove of a consonant that cuts both ways, but it doesn't make an attractive opening sound—the weird spike of the double-*l*, the open ending. Now pronounce the mellifluous tones of *chartreuse*—the powerfully soft assertion of the *cha*, the labial click of the *rt*, followed by another *r*, the *rtr* combination in the center like a worn old mountain, leveling out into the plains of a deceptive diphthong—in fact, it's a straightforward *u* sound in English, but just having that *e* precede it orthographically makes it silkier in the mind and in the mouth—and the water landing of the *s*. Not to mention the French etymological canopy, a guaranteed charm for the English. Yellow shows its Saxon roots.)

But as soon as the trim and bookshelves were done in the darker color, merely the next bar on the paint chit, it all came right. Delicious. My study, where I would work—think hard, read close, write through my agonies. No *yellow wallpaper*, this.

Chartreuse.

❧

Gopnik has no words of his own to finish his article, but rather quotes Freud, on losing his beloved daughter: *We know that the acute sorrow we feel after such a loss will run its course, but also that we will remain inconsolable . . . And that is how it should be.*

❧

"Green is both envy and hope," Alexander Theroux says the novelist James McCourt once told him. *"And who can tell them apart?"*

❧

Summer passed into fall, when fall things were supposed to happen: New school year, theater season. Elections.

P tuned in to Cadabra plays. The worst was a musical murder mystery by Broadway stars brought to the brink of desperation by a lack of audience: linked selfie videos setting to rest any doubts that the skill sets required by stage versus screen were very different. Richard Nelson's Apple Family plays were promising, but mostly just an essentialization of what all the middle-class people were going through—why tune in to that?

Ironically, one of the best was local, by Fayetteville's sole professional company, TheatreSquared, whose brand new facility, opened just last year, P could almost see from her study, not that *near* or *far* were useful words anymore. *Russian Troll Farm: A Workplace Comedy*—daring, pernicious, paranoid; the story of post-Soviet techsters incentivized to get inside Americans' heads and tell them what to think.

P could tell it was good but, unfortunately, within minutes found she could no longer keep her eyes open, at 8:00 p.m. on a not-tiring day. It was the lead-up to the presidential election, and P's best guess was a stress-induced narcolepsy. (Once, on a long-haul bus in India, going round hairpin bends at sixty miles per hour on a narrow mountain road, she had been unable to keep awake. Her astonished friend later described having wrapped P's T-shirt in her fist as insurance: "There was nothing on the windows. You just flopped right out there.")

She loved the new At Home section that replaced Travel in the Sunday *Times*, especially the recipes and the word games, both quick and easy: a guaranteed route to accomplishing something in under an hour. Otherwise, days stretched until they snapped: from the vantage point of morning, the day loomed endless; you moved forward into it with too many tasks and tons of time and then suddenly it was over. They all showered and changed or not or not. P knew now she only needed to dress from the waist up for teaching, with eyeliner and earrings, which she liked the look of in her Cadabra window. Her hair got long, while Mac, smugly, kept to the routine he'd had for almost fifteen years, shaving his own head with clippers. Deepa learned to barber and kept Aakash looking neat with a cut every three weeks.

P was first attacked while trimming her own dry ends. She had watched a couple of YouTube videos on technique: parting it in the back, she pulled the hair over her shoulders, then gathered a triangular section at the front into a ponytail. She bent forward over the sink and started snipping at it, when her breath started turning ragged, more and more, until it was like someone punching her with increasing force in the diaphragm. She stopped cutting, put the scissors down carefully, feeling that she couldn't judge the height or distance of the counter. Her vision purpled and popped at its edges like film burning in a projector. She stumbled with her arms out to the bed, felt her way onto it, and curled up as the assault spread to the area around her jugular. Her throat closed and opened in pulses.

"Mom!" she heard. Deepa calling for her. "Mom!" P gulped for breath, tried to respond. "Where's Mom?" Deepa asked, in the living room, just on the other side of the wall. P, facing away from the door on the edge of the bed, couldn't make herself flip over. She heard someone come in the open door, pause, go out again.

The faint texturing of the wall stood out in relief until she started seeing images in it as if in clouds—a frowning face that morphed into a smiling one that morphed into a presidential sneer. The soft cotton of the Indian quilt clutched in her unmoving fingers resolved into a thousand individual textures she'd never noticed; the spines of the books on the bedside table—Merwin, Larkin, Hass, Wilbur; she'd been sleeping poorly, and thought poetry might help, but Larkin, especially, did not—seemed to telegraph messages. All the heightened significance was terrifying: was she dying?

Then, all at once, her tracheal accordion released in a long atonal wheeze. She drew breath and, in another astonishing narcoleptic release, fell asleep.

Two hours later, she stumbled out, past all her family members, all hypnotized by the pendulums of their devices.

"When's dinner?" Aakash asked as she passed him.

It was almost 6:30, but clearly no one had started cooking nor thought to wonder why she hadn't. Her mouth was stuck together with what tasted like envelope glue, her vision still hyperreal in patches, blurry in others. *Just like our life,* she supposed, sighing through her nose and getting a glass of water.

No one asked and so she didn't say anything, until later that night, when she named it to Mac: "I think I had a panic attack earlier today."

"What?" He looked over and then back at his screen. "When?"

"Around 4:00? What did you guys think I was doing in here?"

"Deepa said you were napping."

"I was in the middle of it when she came in, but she couldn't tell, and then I napped after it passed."

He closed his computer. "How do you know that's what it was?"

Because who wasn't having panic attacks right now? "That's what it felt like."

He opened his computer again. "What did it feel like? Women get diagnosed with panic disorder at twice the rate of men, with real physical problems getting overlooked."

"It was a panic attack," she insisted.

He looked over at her and sighed. "Hon, it's your body. But you should see a doctor, make sure it's not, I don't know, a lung condition."

"I know a lung condition I can get by going to the emergency room," she said huffily, picking up a book from her bedside table: Elizabeth Bishop.

He made an impatient noise. "Why the emergency room? Just call your doctor."

"Or I could do what you were about to do—look up my symptoms—which I did already."

Mac stood. "As I said, your body. But you don't want to be gaslighting yourself if it's something real." He went into the bathroom and started the shower.

She cast an irritated glance at the closed door, a glance that somehow also took in the contents of his screen: he had been working on his resume again, apparently. His tenure materials were due in a couple of weeks, so it might be for that, or for a new gig, or a conference. He had lots of good reasons to work on his resume. But she was surprised to see on it the name of a company that had gone bankrupt about five years earlier. Before that happened, they had reached out to Mac and put him through several revisions of a proposal that never got past that stage. She remembered it because it pissed him off, and rightly so, but what was it doing on his resume under "Consulting," then? He'd never been paid, as far as she knew: was this a way of paying himself back for the work?

She scrolled down. This was the Projects section, a thick block he had, rightly, put ahead of his relatively skinny list of Publications. She spotted two other gigs she knew had fallen through, with relatively obscure outfits, back in New York. It's not like anyone could check on them, and the proposals alone were a lot of work, but: not the same as execution.

She heard the water turn off, shifted the computer to face away from her, went back to her book. Mac came out, silhouetted in the remnants of bathroom steam. He reached for his laptop, saying, "I've got a couple of things to finish up. You can turn out the lights." She heard him settle on the couch, just on the other side of the wall from her.

She woke when he came in a few hours later, and listened to him fall asleep while she remained on some kind of high alert. Finally, she got up, went out, walked past his computer, lying invitationally on the coffee table, made a cup of tea, walked back to it, knowing without letting herself think it that she was going to take a closer look at his resume. Such a thing would never have occurred to her before, but his small lie had somehow given her permission. It was her future, too, after all.

But when she opened the computer—she guessed his new password easily, their deceased cat plus the last four digits of his phone (who was it that said we should just name our pets after our passwords?)—it wasn't his resume that was open, but a photos file full of pictures of young women, on campus, in the grocery store. Each woman featured in a series of five or six shots, starting far away and moving closer. They were not posing; they didn't know they were being photographed.

Okay, she thought, *okay,* feeling her pulse and breath quicken in ways that, in contrast to that afternoon, were wholly explicable. She knew what he would say if she asked. She had been with him when he had taken pictures in restaurants or hotels, people, mostly women, sitting in chairs. He worked on the interaction of people—well, mostly women—with the built environment. He'd say he was taking notes. But if she had ever seen him photographing a single woman, a single woman over and over, she hadn't known. Hadn't realized. Still, she would have asked him about the file, deflected his questions about what she was doing looking in his computer, maybe even pressed him, which he never took well, but maybe she would have had the courage if she hadn't found the pictures of herself.

The pictures, as I have said, seemed mostly to be of young women. If they weren't young, they were at least slim, fit. There was not a great diversity of female body types in the photos. And they were mostly stationary—sitting or standing, highlighting a textbook in a study lounge, leaning against a wall waiting to get into a classroom. There was one exception to this, and it was pictures of P: getting on her bike outside Old Main, walking out of Kimpel Hall, checking in at the gym in the Union. These were all photos from 2020, but the file went back years and years—photos of women in New York City, and P (harried: waiting for a bus, entering a bakery); photos of women from six weeks they spent in Paris, and P (pregnant: entering an archives, reading Houelle-becq on a bench by the Seine); photos of women in Montreal, and P (crossing the campus, eating a bag lunch under a tree); photos of women across Canada during a bicycle trip Mac had done the summer before starting at McGill; photos of women in Bloom-ington, Indiana, where Mac had lived before Montreal.

All of it was disconcerting, but none so much as the photos of P in Montreal from the year *before* she and Mac met.

The computer scrambled dates on the older photos—one set was labeled 1980. But she could date them because there were shots of her in Au Scar Sauvage, a body modification parlor and tea shop in the Gay Village, a place that had closed down before she met Mac. She knew this because she had regretted not being able to take him there.

Now she saw herself back on that terrasse, taking a seat in one of the uncomfortable wrought-iron chairs; ordering lunch, sipping a caffè latte, reading Hélène Cixous. She still had that volume and knew its cover like the back of her own hand, she thought, zooming in on the cover and the back of her own hand.

She paged forward to the most recent set of pictures, back through twenty-five years of her and other women, forward again. She heard Mac turn over in bed, quickly closed his computer and picked up that day's At Home section of the *Times*. She had saved the last word game, intending it as a treat for the next day. She figured she could use that treat now: Building Blocks, Will Shortz branching out, three puzzles, each a nine by eight grid: eight words of nine letters, where you were given a block of either the first or middle or last three letters. Beneath each grid was a little flock of three letter sequences, two of which together completed each word. The bonus was that nine letters—three of the sequences—would remain and could be combined to form a clue to a phrase reading down two of the columns in the completed grid.

WHA TAJ OKE had remained on completing the first, a clue to BURST OUT LAUGHING.

RUN NYN OSE was left below ALLERGIC REACTION. The clues were really unnecessary, just a bonus: their true function was as red herrings, making it a little tougher to find the useful pairs; once those were eliminated, the sixteen-letter phrases were obvious in their contexts. Maybe their other function was creating a little more fun for the game-maker.

She started on the third.

She married a stalker?

She opened Mac's computer again, couldn't bear to look, closed it again.

She married her own stalker?

But look, she told herself as the letter sequences started to resolve into words, if she'd never found the file—if she hadn't been snooping, because of her own insecurity—what difference would it have made? None. In their day-to-day, Mac was caring, accountable, available, encouraging. Right? Their story of their meeting was what he told her: that he had noticed her in the McGill library and taken the table beside hers, found an excuse to talk to her. How else would they have met? She hadn't been looking for romance. He took the lead. They'd had a great life together so far, and were still having that life. He was her best friend.

Mostly, the letter sequences were nonsensical. UGN. EQU. Some had semantic content. RED. RUM.

What about all the other women?

Did she need to think about that? Nothing had happened. So he took pictures: there was no evidence that he had even talked to any of the women except her. There was no evidence of anything bad. Was there? No: she had another look. After they met, there were pictures of the two of them, then the three of them, then four, many of them familiar, since he had shared them with P. And then there were the pictures of P he hadn't shared with her, and the pictures of the other women, all taken without their knowledge. Clearly, he didn't expect anyone to look; it's not as though there were selfies of him with any of those women in a motel or something.

She navigated back to the file he'd been on, then shut the laptop and went back to the puzzle. She was close now. Only seven letter sequences left, then five, then three.

She finished. In two vertical columns, she read: ONLY TIME WILL TELL.

The three remaining letter sequences scurried into order: STA YTU NED.

❧

Look at your room late in the evening when you can hardly distin-guish between colours any longer—and now turn on the light and paint what you saw earlier in semi-darkness.—How do you compare the colours in such a picture with those of the semi-dark room?—LUDWIG WITTGENSTEIN, *Remarks on Colour*

❧

P offered to proofread Mac's tenure materials for him, a way to let him either talk to her about the resume-padding or delete it, but he said his colleague would, a more senior faculty member charged with mentoring him through the process. P knew how that worked. The colleague would read it quickly. If anyone fur-ther down the line checked on details, it would be the big com-panies they'd call, the known ones, the prominent ones. That was good, though, right? His references would be solid.

And who didn't pad? She recalled seeing the tenure applica-tion of another colleague, boasting that her students had received certain fellowships that the English department granted annually without fail. Any English professor could claim the students, but this was a detail no one outside of the department was likely to know. The boast was fundamentally true and constitutionally meaningless.

Like our marriage, went the voice. Ugh. She clutched her head, then released, straightened, and downed the last of her Pouilly-Fumé.

ॐ

The panic attacks recurred, five days apart, four, three, two . . . and back to six. Always in the afternoon. She made a note in her diary. She wondered who to call. A therapist? She'd read about therapy going online, but the prospect of trying to find someone locally, vetting therapists over Cadabra, exposing and plumbing her problems over a platform whose security she didn't trust—could she really talk about Mac without an assurance of privacy? And what about privacy from Mac: what if he heard her?—froze her in the amber a whole new level of anxiety.

But everyone was in this amber: kids no longer seeing friends, teachers no longer seeing students, they were all in suspended animation, everyone waiting for the great thaw—a vaccine. No, dummy: amber doesn't suspend you alive, and it doesn't thaw. Except, was it the metaphor that was faulty, or the expectation, that things could ever go back to the way they were? After all, time didn't work that way. They were being transformed, even now, as surely as they ever were, individually, societally. The difference was that now they had much more time to ruminate on how.

She and the kids were watching *Schitt's Creek*. A stinkbug whizzed past her head and smacked into the bookshelf. The children's schools had decided it was just cruel to try to teach any new material, so their minds, in a way, were being mummified. Scarabs in amber. Her mind drifted. Honey had been uncorked three thousand years after being entombed with pharaohs, still golden, still sweet. She sipped her third glass of wine, the dinner dishes done. The panic attacks never happened while she was drinking—coincidence? She felt louche, connected to the world by multiple, indirect, taut and crossing lines. Bees were the original hive mind: who else could have figured out an edible that would last through millennia? There was no single author; there could never be.

Deepa lay on the sofa, Aakash sitting on the floor in front of her. He leaned his head back and Deepa put her fingers in his hair, stroking his head thoughtlessly as, onscreen, the Rose family members all embarrassed themselves and each other entirely in private, in their shared motel room in the middle of nowhere: no witnesses, no audience, no one to know but them.

P was worried about the kids.

When she was thirteen, she had gone to India alone with her father and sister. Her father's mother had started her long death. P's own mother was taking an exam for specialization or something—she couldn't come, is the point—and before they left, she had a talk with P: don't let any of your cousins try to touch you inappropriately. "Indian kids don't date," she said, "so they might be curious about a Western girl."

None of them did, but P saw two older teenage cousins, in one of the many group gatherings, the boy lying with his head in the girl's lap, the girl stroking his hair. She had no other clues, nor did she talk to anyone about it—what was there to say?—but at some later point, her mother made reference to her father having heard of "sexual experimentation" between his own cousins, attributing it to the fact that they didn't have access to the other sex, growing up. It was the inevitable effect of a closed system.

But nothing needed to be traumatic if it wasn't stigmatized: it wasn't the private action that was traumatic, it was the public exposure—iron won't rust unless it's exposed to air.

She recalled Jan Morris on incest, in *Pleasures of a Tangled*

Life, the very book that, later that year, when Morris died, her obituary writer would recommend as a starting place for the uninitiated (making P feel proprietary even though this was the only Morris book she herself had read). Morris is unreliable on the topic of incest, something to do with her being Welsh, or so she says, an island nation within an island nation. (*Island*, from the Old English *igland*, for watery place, had its spelling modified on collision with French, so to bring it closer to *isle*, a word derived from the Latin *insula*, isolated. A reverse-engineered linguistic coincidence.)

Morris mentions an elderly widower in her neighborhood, hauled to jail for sexual relations with his unmarried adult daughter. *I was not alone in thinking it a mean-spirited response to a primitive expression of affection which . . . far from being the cruel abuse of one by the other, undoubtedly brought comfort to them both.*

Morris herself confesses to having conceived, when her kids were small, the *outrageous whim* that her daughter would marry her son, *made for each other.* It seemed a limited idea of complementarity, especially strange given that Morris, born a man, and her wife stayed together even after her transition. But it's what most of us know: Aakash had thought, when he and Deepa were tiny, that they would be a married couple when they grew up. It made sense—they shared a room, just as P and Mac did, to all appearances a couple in the making.

But as with the Indian cousins, Morris's kids, she says somewhat ruefully, *made more ordinary arrangements of their own.*

P watched her children move about the house, their orbits colliding, intersecting, pulling apart. The isolation, the insularity. Who would blame them? P? Never. But would they blame themselves? Would this comfort rust into trauma if and when it came to light?

Sexual release, we say, but it had never been more obvious that release usually meant nothing more than escape into a bigger box.

Other days, she shook her head and wanted to slap herself. What kind of person would suspect her children of such horror! She had no proof. Whereas with Mac, she'd had no suspicions, but now had plenty of proof.

But proof of what?

She withdrew from him, watched him, her paranoia festering, spending longer and longer hours in her study. "You're working a lot," Mac observed, and she murmured agreement but the lie was double-padded: she was on deadline for a translation of 2019's runner-up to Quebec's biggest book prize, but was neglecting that almost entirely in favor of her essay.

What had begun as an entertainment had opened like an ornate folding screen (*an oriental screen!* cackled that voice in her head): a refuge from the pandemic became also a reflection on the pandemic, and, eventually, a sort of tarot: she could not tell whether she was following or creating the chains of association, but either way, the writing was guiding her, revealing what she needed to know, so that her hours up on the third floor were, increasingly, more believable and legible than anything to be encountered in the shared stories below.

Above all: the demons of her self-loathing didn't follow her up here. They were dogging her in the mornings now—no, dogging was a bad verb. Dogs want to please; her demons wanted to demonize. People thought demonizing was something that the righteous did, but that was wrong. It was what a vampire or zombie did to induct you into their uncanny army, the way, in *Lovecraft Country*, little Diana's demons dance and prance and scratch and snatch at her. P knew her own demons were the products of her own mind: Did that mean she was to blame? Did it mean she was not to blame?

It used to be, as she emerged from sleep into the morning's dark or half-light, that dreams kept the demons at bay, at least until she could get to her desk, but more and more often now, she wakened to find they were already there, perched on the edges of her mind, knock-knock-knockin' at her noggin, telling her all the things she already knew:

So pretentious, so needlessly ambitious, so blind: you're an awful person.

You're abandoning your kids to their own devices—literally. And for what—your "work?"

Why do most people think you're smart? Because they're even dumber than you. It's only when you're around a truly brilliant person that your true dullness shows: that's why such people don't speak to you, and why you're tongue-tied around them. Stupid. Worthless.

The demons chased her in the floors below, but fell away as she started up the perilously steep stairs to her chartreuse room. In her study, she knew that famous people ignored her at festivals and events because they were narcissistic and mobbed by sycophants, and that she was quiet out of nervousness and an aversion to throngs.

In her study, she thought about other things, interesting things.

Meanwhile, the demons waited at the bottom of the stairs, inhaling their own rancid breath, filing their nails to points.

It made her want to avoid the stairs. It made her want to find another way out.

ॐ

What green room doesn't try to evoke a bower of bliss, call up nature's green hills, mime the verdant glade? It is, half the time, almost a state of mind. —ALEXANDER THEROUX, *The Secondary Colors*

ॐ

One day, she and Mac rode their bikes up to Lake Fayetteville. P had been exercising at home, living-room Pilates every two days, but Mac had always been less consistent about working out. He would sign up for CrossFit or install a pull-up bar, practicing with mad intensity for a few months, extolling the activity, crowing about how good he felt, before letting it, inevitably, fade away. Now, lacking new outlets, he was getting a bit soft.

They paused for water on the high berm that formed one side of the lake. To their right, a couple of college-age women sat on a bench and laughed. Mac looked over at them and P looked over at him. "Going to take a picture?"

He turned to her, his eyes shuttering but not before she glimpsed his fear. "What do you mean? Why would I?"

P was appalled: this was not like her. This kind of standoff was fun to watch in *Mr. and Mrs. Smith* or *The Blacklist*, but it was no way to live, not in real life. She gestured vaguely toward the lake and stuck her water bottle in her mouth as one would a cigar or breast.

Mac shook his head, vaguely, and swigged from his bottle, too.

It was a quiet ride home. And a quiet dinner. *So not like me,* she kept hearing herself say, more and more pleased at having done it.

That night, P rooted around in her sock drawer, looking for cotton socks to wear to bed. The weather had started to cool. Her hand closed on nylon. There in her palm were all the sockettes she'd been missing since spring. How odd she didn't find them before. True, they were out of place in this drawer but it was a drawer she had used plenty in these months, burrowing and over-turning piles of socks for working out, for walks, for sleep. She would have seen them had they been here all along.

She mentioned it to Mac when she went to bed. "I found those sockettes!" He glanced over from his computer. "The nylons I'd been missing."

"Okay," he said, as though he had no idea what she meant and was, appropriately, uninterested. And yet she felt a signal, from him, as though he were a satellite receiver invisibly beaming back her own paranoiac fears. A frisson of defeat, whose counterpart in her was a frisson of victory.

A couple of days later, against all odds—this is not a cliché, because it's not figurative but arithmetical—Mac got sick.

It started with a sniffle, and developed into a sore throat, hacking cough, and honking nose, congestion as though he were backed up all the way into his lungs and beyond, his whole thorax and whatever organs it contained. Oh, right: his *heart*. Maybe he had a congestive heart. Maybe it was to blame for his failures.

He got tested for COVID-19, or so he claimed.

It wasn't COVID-19, or so he claimed.

He hadn't been in contact with anyone. Or so he claimed.

He had, of course, gone to the protests. Mac had never missed an opportunity to show solidarity with social justice. He wore a mask, though usually below his nose. Anyway, contrary to everyone's fears, the protests didn't super-spread. Eventually they learned that the virus was really hard to catch outside, especially if you were masked, which most protesters were.

P heard a *This American Life* episode, "Cold Case," in which Nadia Reiman's husband gets a cold, even despite their family's rigorous social isolation *mostly for his sake*: he's immunocompromised in the respiratory system. *That's husbands for you,* P thought as she listened.

On the episode, a specialist gave them several possible explanations, the most convincing being that the husband was attacked by a bacterial infection, bacteria that had been with him the whole time but was strengthened and enabled by their newly sterile environment.

The call had been coming from within the house. RED RUM.

Still, better the devil you know. Especially when the alternative was COVID-19.

Mac might be telling the truth. Chances are he was. But he wasn't truthful. What was he full of, if not truth? *He was full of shit.*

Until now, she had quelled that voice, let her demons gabble over it, drown it out. They were not quiet now, but they were chastened somewhat. That voice: not like her. Unless it was? What if it was *very like* her?

Because Mac was sick, she started sleeping on the narrow daybed in her study.

She had only ever worked up there; she slept and dreamed in the bedroom, beside Mac. Now work and dreams meshed. She wrote, she read, she conjured. She drank wine in the evening, she lay abed in the morning, imagining someone *very like* herself but less lonely, more independent, more angry, more maternal, more fun.

Conjure: from Latin to Old French to Middle English: to band together by oath, to call up by magic.

And as this other self bodied forth, P began to feel she herself was being conjured out of ether and oaths, by herself, by some other P—what was the difference?—and so to wonder whether these two could be one traveler.

P2 Fall to Spring

The trees are coming into leaf
Like something almost being said;
The recent buds relax and spread.
Their greenness is a kind of grief

—PHILIP LARKIN, *"The Trees"*

AND THEN THE earth shuddered to a halt. She saw the map in her mind's eye, starting in Wuhan and spreading, spreading. A stillness, fanned out in uneven waves, like an invisible knife frosting a cake, except that each stroke of the knife made its impasto thicker and wider at once.

But there was no need to resort to metaphor. The earth literally had been stilled: COVID-19 shutdowns led to *the longest and most coherent global seismic noise reduction in recorded history*, the *Times* said scientists said.

Mat, beside her, stirred, opened an arm, and P moved in and laid her head on his chest. It wasn't a position she'd ever found comfortable, her ear ridges against the ridges of his ribs, but he loved it and she let her head fill with the beat of his steady heart, ignoring her own for a few minutes. They had turned a corner. The marriage, the earth: both appeared as though they might hang on a bit longer.

The dog butted open the door, the cat ran past him and jumped on the bed and the dog, thinking that gave him permission, jumped up after the cat, landing heavily with one paw upon

Mat's crotch, so that he bolted upright and tossed everyone off. He curled into fetal position.

This was July.

♦

The previous October, the two of them had attended a celebration for recently promoted faculty members. One of those (a pompous but goodhearted classicist) had just climbed a rung to Distinguished Professor. Now he came over to them, wearing his medal, as if towed by his own wide smile from across the room. Raising his glass to return their toast, he said, "Your turn next year, eh, Mat?"

Indeed it looked that way. Mat was flabbergasted at this prospect. P didn't see why: he'd produced a book a year for fifteen years, among them an anthology of twentieth century French poetry so inclusive that it made Paul Auster's appear to belong to another century altogether. He'd won most of the most competitive literary fellowships in the country, in addition to various prizes. Yet he still saw himself as a diffident Vermonter—blunts, Bob Dylan, tie-dye—a hippie, and the child of hippies, who themselves had been the children of factory workers and schoolteachers. His people were rough or genteel, but none had turned the cranks of power. Boasting wasn't in their blood. (Mat's father Lon had risen the furthest before Mat himself: also a distinguished poet, but raised by a single mom, he had a bit of a tendency to boastful narcissism, which had made Mat all the more diffident.)

Mat's accomplishments made P happy, and proud. Why shouldn't she be? She told him she was. He deserved all of it. Except that October was the same month when she applied, year after year, for all those same fellowships, without success. She wouldn't have called herself bitter, but there was some kind of taste in her mouth. She sipped at her wine and rinsed it behind her teeth.

♦

She'd enjoyed these academic drinks affairs when they first moved to Fayetteville, when Nikhil and Sarojini were small and her first novel was not yet published. People were kind, and interested in her; she and Mat hadn't yet found the friends they would end up keeping. She had been browsing, in a way. Before too long, she learned Fayetteville had a high density of interesting people—she was as likely to meet kindred spirits at the public library or park playground—and got tired of the university events, of bracing herself for the inevitable microaggression while clutching a glass of cabernet served up by two of the six brown-and-Black people in the room (a third would take her glass when she was done; the remainder would be faculty members she knew).

What mostly made the events tolerable were colleagues who had become friends. She stood with two of them now, balancing canapés and making cracks: Ximena, an architect who, years ago, even before P was tenure track, had invited her onto a committee programming interdisciplinary diversity speakers, and Gal, whom P had met at an event much like this one during P's first year on the tenure track.

At that party, P had slid into one of the only empty seats in the room, across from a squat man in a bow tie. He leaned on a cane and extolled the difficulties of editing some journal. "And the articles from India! The extra articles in the articles." He moued.

"They put an *a* or *the* in front of every noun, proper or improper."
Oh, the grammar, the usage, the extra work. The prepositional
errors alone!

P didn't think his anecdote was provoked by her arrival. His
glance slid past her as he spoke, his remarks seeming almost
rehearsed. Maybe he went ahead despite her appearance at the
table, so as not to waste his practice. Should she say something?
Indian English is *an English dialect—you wouldn't fault Brits for
writing 'at the weekend.'* But he was just a little too far away (big
table) and she hadn't been invited to respond and by the time
she took a breath, the conversation had moved on. She swept her
glance around the others at the table and made eye contact with
someone she'd seen around campus, also in a bow tie and vest,
as it happened, but natty, androgynous, à la garçonne, an air of
irony and compact readiness. Gal, as they turned out to be called,
made a face at P, widened eyes, flared nostrils, and P snorted. The
two of them got up and commingled outrage over a Sterno vat of
stuffed mushrooms. Gal had many more horror stories and told
them better.

It was Ximena, a veteran academic, who had helped P debrief
her failure to make the shortlist the first time she applied for a
tenure-track position in creative writing at the University of
Arkansas; the finalists were three white men with accomplishments comparable to her own. (The next year, the program's
director, who'd been outvoted, campaigned vigorously for P to be
taken on as a spousal hire.)

It was Gal who convened a covert faculty resistance group after
the 2016 election, a loose network that gathered to trade stories
and concerns and tips on assisting traumatized Black and Latinx
and Muslim and queer students. (The chancellor's office, getting
wind of it, invited them to come for a meeting and then didn't

follow up on any of their suggestions or requests, making them wonder exactly how stupid they'd been to step out of the shadows of their anonymity.)

They were soldiers in a fight for territory whose borders they drew day after day, or woke to see drawn against them. It was a good fight and P was glad to be some small part of it, except that of course they all wished they didn't have to fight, but this was the U of A in the US of A and they did.

The question was how to live day-to-day. P thought a lot about others' marriages: Ximena was a first-generation Nicaraguan, married to the scion of a Little Rock family of Black lawyers and doctors. As a couple, they had agreed to steer clear of Oppression Olympics, but the complications of their dynamics seemed articulable, at least from the outside. Gal's wife was a mousy Lebanese woman who taught in Tulsa; she did little but smile enigmatically the few times P met her, but Gal fawned over her and became, if anything, more voluble when she was around.

What did it mean that P's spouse was a straight white man? Not to mention a writer? (How did Claudia Rankine manage? Zadie Smith? If only P could know.)

P and Mat had met at a dinner party in Montreal when he was doing his PhD and she was still with her first husband. Throughout that evening, they carefully suppressed their mutual electric awareness. When, after virtually simultaneous divorces, they met up again by coincidence, at an artists' residency in New Hampshire, it seemed like fate.

She had never felt so free, so uncensored, not with anyone. Mat had some kind of calming effect, not just on her. One of her best friends, whose stutter had tightened into muteness around P's judgmental first husband, became animated and jokey with Mat. When Mat met P's sister's cat, an animal that had always comported itself with a violent chthonic rage, it fell asleep purring in his lap.

Sometimes P felt as if, in the years after moving to the United States and having children, she had awakened from such a spell, been lured south for love and then shook her head and blinked and found herself a stranger in a strange land.

Not Arkansas. Her marriage.

Although the problem, really, was that it was increasingly hard to tell those apart.

♦

A week or two after that university reception, P and Mat went to see a touring production of *Cabaret* at the performing arts center. She felt faintly possessive, a dash of vinegar in her brain fluid: she had worshipped Isherwood's fey mordant style since she was young, whereas Mat knew him only as Auden's boyfriend. Chatting in the theater afterward, as they gathered their things, she moved quickly toward a structural reading that he resisted, maybe because the curtain had just fallen and he needed more time to think, maybe because there was a specious aspect to her arguments, along with a detectable pugnaciousness in her delivery. Anyway, she got fed up. She said she wanted to walk home.

She had dressed for date night, dressed for Mat, in high sexy boots and a swingy vintage jacket over tight pants. Fortunately, the boots were made for walking: Fluevogs furnished thick rubber soles, even with heels. She stalked up Dickson Street, cooled by winter air and an exhilarated relief. She had never walked out on an argument, always wanting to talk things through. He was the sort to leave, slam the door, saying, *I can't talk about this right now*, but the problem was that, at least early on, she thought that meant he'd let her know when he was ready to talk. He never did, and if she brought up the fight after he calmed down, he would accuse her of rehashing, of hoarding her anger, after he had magnanimously let his go. She needed to understand their differences, she said. He thought they should get on with things, not waste time fighting. But fights happen anyway, she argued, shouldn't they try to learn from them? Wouldn't they get worse otherwise? Then they would metafight, fight about how they fought, exhaust themselves before they could ever get to the problem itself. Unless that *was* the problem?

It seemed to her that Merwin's Berryman's apocryphal dictum about writing applied equally to marriage: *I asked how can you ever be sure / that your marriage is really any good at all / and he said you can't / you can't you can never be sure / you die without knowing / whether anything you tried was any good / if you have to be sure, don't marry.*

There were crowds on the street downtown in the entertainment district but as soon as she crossed College Avenue into the residential zone, she was alone. In Montreal, there had always been people out, walking home from dinner parties, bars, shows. In Fayetteville, people walked to their cars. Once or twice before, she'd tried to walk home after a night out with girlfriends, but been exquisitely aware of her vulnerability, even jumped behind a bush once to hide from approaching headlights. Ridiculous: there was virtually no street crime here, maybe two or three anonymous assaults annually, tops. Rapes mainly happened in frat houses. But it was no fun to be the only person walking after dark; it did things to your head.

Minutes later, a guy in a truck pulled alongside and started talking to her through his open window, creeping along beside her. "No," she told him. Was he being kind, worried, offering a ride? Or aggressive, wanting to pick her up? She wouldn't know, wouldn't look at him. "Fuck off!" she cried, her voice choked with frustration. "Leave me alone." Then she saw their old car just ahead, idling, pulled over, a safety trap. Mat waited within, patient and uncertain. She got in, like a child talked out of running away from home, and now the tears came in floods and fury: "All I wanted to do was to walk home, be alone, let my head sort itself out, and fucking Arkansas doesn't even let me do that."

"Yes," Mat said. "I'm sorry, I know." It didn't help, his sympathy. It didn't change anything. To be able to rage up her own street in peace—was it too much to ask?

↓

Daily, they both rode their bikes to the university, but only she got catcalls, mostly in spring. Once, a carful of young men screamed and hooted at her as they passed her and then got stopped at a light. She caught up and berated them through the window—"You're yelling at me riding up hill while you're sitting on your asses in your daddy's SUV?"—relishing their mortification.

Whenever she posted on social media about such incidents, though, male cyclist friends responded—assuming she, like them, had been abused for being on a bicycle, and there was something to that.

At a state park session on Arkansas reptiles, once, their family had learned that drivers swerve to avoid turtles but swerve to hit snakes. As snake lovers, Nik and Saro had taken this personally, but, as cyclists, Mat and P's conversation afterward jumped a track onto evidence that drivers made a similar distinction between pedestrians and bikes. People hit pedestrians all the time but they didn't mean to. Arkansas drivers might have some crosswalk blindness, but bikes made them see red. Why? Maybe cycling looked too fun. P thought she must radiate smugness when she cruised past a traffic jam: thick, static lines of cars, drivers marinating in exhaust fumes and their own lack of imagination as she threaded elegantly to the front, singing to herself. Pity the poor commuter.

She loved steaming uphill to the campus, sometimes past her own students. The downside was coming to class sweaty, but it was worth it to project the badassness she gathered on the way up that hill.

Whoever knew what people actually saw, though? People saw Mat as a "distinguished prof"—definitely not how he saw himself. And P? She'd learned that students and many of their friends, and even Mat, saw her as tough. She thought of herself as wimpy.

People also saw her as brown, which still surprised her, every time she was introduced to a white liberal who namasted her with that eager look predictive of tales of travels in India.

Liberals such as the owner of her yoga studio, who, at a party, asked P, "But what do you call yourself? How do you identify?" Her husband was talking loudly with P's dad, gesturing with one of the bespoke cocktails that had begun to slur yoga-lady's speech.

P shrugged: "Canadian?" Always that little push or pull. No one who asked where she was from ever took Canada for an answer.

"But, *Canadian*," the woman said, like it was a foreign word she knew how to pronounce authentically (*sauvignon blanc, bruschetta* . . .), "that's Caucasian, right? So . . ."

P was proud of herself for walking away.

"She's weird," Mat said, dismissing it, when she told him the story.

"Only to have said it," P pointed out. "They all think it." He nodded, and she conceded, "Though you're right that she's weird." (The woman emailed the next day with a vague apology, blaming it on the drink. "Happens all the time," P responded.)

Previously, Mat had mildly defended such questions, acknowledging that they were othering, but also pointing out that people were honestly curious. P could agree on that: anytime their family heard an accent or language they didn't immediately recognize, they were riveted, speculating and eavesdropping, hoping for a clue.

This time, though, there was no way around the offense. Since this kind of thing never happened with their actual friends, P had learned it was best to avoid meeting new people their actual friends hadn't vetted.

Harder to avoid were work and wifedom. She had followed Mat to Arkansas when he got the job here but, after her first novel was published to reasonable success, she took a half-time job as a visiting professor, with hopes she might move onto the tenure track whenever there was an opening. When the opportunity arose, her second novel was in the pipeline and their daughter starting kindergarten—perfect timing. So she threw her hat in the ring, telling her colleagues, who were also Mat's colleagues, that the decision was theirs to make and she would not take it wrong no matter what.

When she was not short-listed, almost as if to prove what a good sport she was, she still attended the candidate dinners as a faculty spouse. (Perhaps she also had some masochistic curiosity; perhaps she wanted to show them she wasn't going away.

Regardless, she allowed Mat to drape his gladness and gratitude over her shoulders like a soft shawl.) At the first of these, excusing herself to the ladies' room, she found herself face-to-face with the MFA program's prestige novelist, a long-ago National Book Award winner, who had once infamously asked another Arkansas colleague how he coped, teaching so many Black students: "In Mississippi, they knew their place," she told him, standing too close. "Here? Uh-uh. They're *overreaching*." Among the MFA students, it was well known that she favored macho fiction by white men. She was a curiosity to P, being in that extreme minority among writers: a Republican.

Now she fingered a lock of P's hair. "Look at you. So pretty." It was how she typically greeted P, but this time, as P fake-smiled and tried to leave, the writer remarked on the reasons P had not been short-listed for the job: "We just want to find what's right for *you*." Later, the creative writing director told P that there'd been talk of finding her an administrative position—the university's technique, historically, for assuaging ambitious wives.

P tried not to dwell. She got her tenure-track position the next year. Irksome that it was a spousal hire; she wondered if that would stigmatize her, but if so, she didn't hear about it. And what was any of this, compared to what her Black and Latinx and queer colleagues and students endured? Middle-class cis-het South Asian Canadians were hardly disadvantaged in academia. P was no Oppression Olympics medalist.

It wasn't a big deal. But it was also not nothing. At some point, the English department head spoke to her about that search. P dismissed it: "They didn't like my books. I don't take it personally."

"That's good," the head responded, a medievalist who surely had seen her share, "because it's not personal. It's structural."

Bingo.

Did P need a white woman to tell her that? It's not as though she didn't understand such matters. She had just always preferred, for her sense of social justice and for her own dignity, to believe they didn't apply to her.

Each insult was a jagged little pebble. They had substance, were pieces of the world they lived in, but she could toss them in a box and get on with her life. It wasn't as though it only happened in Arkansas. It had been happening her whole life: Edmonton, Hamburg, Montreal. For now, though, *it was happening in Arkansas*. And the stones seemed to come at her more often here, in this place where liberals were, as a class, besieged; in the land of Tom Cotton (*so bad they named him after a slave crop,* cackled one of their friends) and concealed carry, where the stakes of being labeled *other* were higher, and starker.

Now, after fifteen years here, the box was so full it wouldn't even rattle when she shook it.

Most of all, she worried about their kids, what effect being raised in Arkansas would have on them. Since birth, she'd taken a rigorously antisexist line with them, an attitude they might have imbibed with the water if they'd stayed in the Bay Area, not that that was ever an option.

Nikhil asked for nail polish when he was four. Three girls in his preschool collared him to inform him this was Not Allowed. In first grade, over the winter break, he let P paint his nails in alternating neon green and royal blue, using the contrasting color to make a race car stripe down the middle of each nail. She hedged when he asked her to take it off before he started school, wanting him to be a little warrior, then felt terrible when she saw him do an entire spelling bee with hands in his pockets.

When Sarojini, at five, asked P's parents for a Barbie for

Christmas, P objected vociferously. Her mother said, "It's what she wants. What should we get her, then?"

"Matchbox cars," P told her, incredulously. "That's what you got Nik."

"Yes, and you criticized us," her mother returned. "*Why are you getting him cars? That's what you said.*"

"One way or another," Mat reasoned, "Saro's going to have to find her own way in this culture."

P finally consented to a Belle doll, because when Belle first appears in *Beauty and the Beast*, she's absorbed in a book. A couple of years later, she and Saro were playing Barbies on the floor of her room. The dolls' number had mysteriously increased to some half a dozen, and P said, "But remember . . ."

"I know, Mommy, I know." Saro was still learning to roll her eyes but never broke the industrial rhythm of dressing and combing and posing the dolls. "*No real woman has those proportions.*"

"Yes," P said weakly. This counted as a victory, right?

"*She'd fall over,*" Saro continued in an uncanny imitation of her mother, as she got several Barbies, improbably, to stand up.

It was reassuring to see, when Saro was tiny, that Mat gave no evidence of shaping his behavior toward her by gender expectations. It wasn't just the obvious matters, roughhousing or clothing choices. He got Saro her own little tool kit, as he had for Nik; fretted over her bicycling skills, as he had over Nik's; insisted they settle on an accurate name for her genitals, one she could grow with, pointing out that American culture didn't readily provide those to girls as it did boys. Was P allowed to paraphrase Pat Parker? *For the white man who wants to know how to be my child's father: The first thing you do is to forget she's a brown girl. Second, you must never forget that she's a brown girl.* Mat would never say he was free from internalized sexism, but it appeared to P that his desire to do right by the kids was incompatible with knuckling them into gender boxes.

How, though, to counteract the culture? *So smart,* people would say about Nikhil, in front of him. "He's going to be an engineer or something," the school secretary marveled.

So pretty, they would say about and to Saro, though Nik was just as gorgeous and Saro just as good in math.

Ultimately, the kids were incontrovertibly gendered. Saro was bad at sports; Nik was bad at dancing. By the age of three, Saro was an "active listener"—emitting sounds and expressions that made people want to tell her more—while Nik was a utilitarian listener, antennae tuned to facts and arguments, not to social cues.

Was that Arkansas, though? Or was it their individual genetic coding in reaction with their environment, fizzing along at the atomic level like copper exposed to the elements?

And how much of it was due to P's own internalized sexism? Once, back in San Francisco, they arrived at a card game to learn that a Stanford buddy of Mat's had just been characterizing her to their circle as the perfect girlfriend. She was flattered—how inane she was to be flattered! It was a trap, she could see that now: it made her want to live up to the epithet. It made her want be the perfect wife.

Before marrying, her only ambitions had ever been to be a writer and a mother. She understood and accepted the sacrifices these entailed. (Or so she wanted to believe, though this might have been hard to confirm in those frequent moments when she complained at top volume about picking up after the kids.) "Wife" was incidental to that. She would have had kids on her own if she hadn't met Mat. So this was the first way she was not a perfect wife: she had never wanted to be a wife at all.

She'd always found weddings embarrassing—the vows, the pictures, the outfits—always scorned those girls and women who fantasized about being a bride. Did men fantasize about weddings? She suspected the contents of their fantasy lives were rather different.

The closest she'd come to thinking it would be a good idea to marry was in speculating when she was young that since she'd grown up in a home presided over by devoted partners, maybe she'd be good at marriage. She learned when her parents came to live with them that there were in fact virtually no lessons she could carry over from their relationship to her own, that gaps of generation, culture, personalities, and priorities made their marriage even less instructive than Mat's parents', who divorced the minute he left home.

Which had meant that for Mat, while he didn't swoon over wedding fashions, he really wanted to be in a committed relationship. He confessed shortly after they got together that his biggest nightmare was ending up like his own father, drifting single, able to charm women into marrying him but unable to convince them to stay. Lacking any other anchor, Lon had followed Mat and P to Fayetteville, and, for more than ten years, lived at a respectful distance, close enough to see the kids a few times a week but far enough to permit him one last failed marriage before, finally, a fatal diagnosis motivated him to buy the house next door. Then it was Mat who accompanied him through the cancer and tantrums and denials of his final year, Mat who adapted the new house for his care, Mat who adopted his big old dog, Mat who held his hand through his last acrid breath.

Lon had adored him, and Mat loved him back in stalwart, complicated ways, but conventions of a nature obscure even to them meant they could not say any of this to each other. Both were poets, each among the most skilled of his generation in giving voice to emotions, yet they were unable to speak these to each other. Instead, they performed a kathakali of masculine norms, their feelings expressed entirely in gestures: Mat built Lon a fence; Lon invited Mat to watch basketball.

The dramaturgy was quasi-legible if you were privy to the code. P found it mysteriously touching, in the way of contemporary opera. She realized that, growing up with a sister, no brothers, and a father who happily allowed her mother to do the emotional heavy lifting, she had somehow come to believe that men *felt less* than women did. Emotion in men, their awareness of their own emotions, their articulations of longing, love, and grief, surprised her. It was a given that men were less expressive. How could it be, then, that most artists throughout history were men? (Leave alone the suppression of women artists; men took up that space.)

"They were exceptional men," volunteered Mat, when she put the question to him.

"No." P dissented immediately, though it was his idea that brought her to her own. "They drank and womanized and counted on their women to keep house for them like all the other men, and still never talked to them or anyone else about the important things. You, your dad: you don't treat women like that, but you put your strange and difficult emotions into poems instead of doing the work to talk to your loved ones about them."

Why? Because no one contravenes what you say in a poem. And because when men put their vulnerability and nuance in their writing, it got them adulation. Expressing themselves to their wives or kids just submerged them further (tied in a sack, weighted with stones) in the hard, ongoing work of making a family and a marriage.

Mat glanced over from his late-night email triage, a look that said *tu as raison*. "You should write that down."

Admittedly, though, P and the babies unlocked something in Lon that he'd wanted to set free: when, near the end of his life, P stopped by one day on her way home from class as she sometimes did, to chat about books and teaching, he said to her, out of the blue, "I've been so lucky, to have lived this long, to have enjoyed the grandchildren, to see Mat succeed as he has. So very fortunate."

Mat was almost jealous: "He never said anything like that to me!"

She didn't say, *Telling you would have broken the rules.*

She didn't say, *You do the same thing.*

♥

She'd been trailing him since they first fell in love. That year, he had gotten a Stegner fellowship at Stanford; his first book of translation came out; he started a second book of translation and published his first book of poems. She followed him to San Francisco and worked on her novel. He published the second translation and got the job in Arkansas. She followed him to Fayetteville and worked on her novel. They bought a house. They had babies. Her parents retired to live with and help them; in Arkansas, she and Mat could afford a house big enough to install her parents on the second floor: two sunny bedrooms and a bathroom just for them, a whole wing hinged onto the rest of the house by the kitchen.

Mat published two more translations plus reams of poems,

got tenure early, and received a Guggenheim fellowship for his anthology. It gave him a year off teaching, but the work of putting together an anthology, it transpired, was agonizing: choosing between poets and versions and translators, the small-*p* politics wringing him dry. He worked on it all the time, but clamored anxiously that he was putting all his time into childcare and chores. This was objectively impossible, P knew, because she kept all-too-close track of how much time each of them, including her parents, spent on kids and chores. She wrote five mornings a week and gave the kids and the house the rest (apart from a moderate daily workout). But she couldn't convince him. Mat was, unlike her, not inclined to bean count. Eventually she would read that a study had proven that modern men consistently and dramatically overestimated the time they spent on household work. Anyway, it was the stress talking.

At some point, she published her novel. It did better than she expected—generous advances in multiple markets, translations into other languages. Apparently an appetite existed for a doorstop historical novel set in an obscure and vanishing Indian subculture. Who knew? She toured internationally. Thank goodness for Mat and her folks. These were the times she felt they were on equal footing, even if she organized everything for her absence, freezing homemade soups and leaving instructional Post-its to grease the household wheels, as Mat would never do when he traveled. He told her not to do it: he cowboy-dadded when he was on his own, did it his way, not hers. She thought hers was better, but his was admittedly less work for both of them. She defrosted the soups herself when she got back.

They invested her book advance in a garage apartment for her folks. Until then, P and her mother had regularly met for combat in the kitchen; now, a little separation reminded them how well they in fact got along. It helped that both her parents were their best selves with the little ones: fun, patient, available. And they enjoyed Lon, as well, falling into a routine together: Friday dinners at his place, Sunday nights in the in-law apartment, Wednesdays at P and Mat's big table. Dinner for seven, three times a week; it made as much work for P as it saved her, but it was worth it. Their neighbors said they should write a sitcom.

That was when P was offered a half-time position, teaching one semester a year. It was optimal: their kids were still small; she was what she had come to call the flex-parent, not stay-at-home, but on-call, managing housework and homework and schedules, groceries and doctors and gymnastics and music lessons.

With a book under her belt, she started applying for the big fellowships alongside Mat. He'd already gotten so many. But now he got The One that she had always dreamed of: the Cullman Center of the New York Public Library. (Cue radiant parting of clouds.)

(Cue crack of thunder.) He hadn't even heard of it when they first met; he first heard of it from her. And now he would live her dream: a year in an office *in* the library at Forty-Second Street. He'd pass the lions every day, caress their stony noses on his way in.

They talked about how to manage. He asked their parents their opinions. Lon and P's folks were in favor, offered to help more: extra grandkid time for them, no complaints. Mat's mother, visiting Fayetteville with her most recent husband, confided to P, "In my generation, a man would never ask. He'd just go." (She often made pithy observations on men's behavior, but to P alone.)

Ultimately, the decision was that P would stay in Arkansas with the kids. Mat would come back for a weekend every two weeks; she and the kids would spend six weeks with him in the fall and two in the spring, when she was teaching. Nik would be in kindergarten, but his school agreed that New York City was a better education and indeed, he would start reading there; Saro would turn three while they were there all together.

They must have come to this arrangement because they thought it would give P the greatest chance at writing her next book. It must have been a mutual decision, not the way some friends later said it looked: a sexist pig leaving his wife in Arkansas with their two young children for a solo year in the Big Apple.

When they visited him, P swallowed chagrin. Absorbing rejection was part of being a writer; she had become adept at it through the years. She took the kids to Central Park and the Met; she brought them to readings and cocktail hours; she befriended the other Cullman Fellows the way she had befriended his Stanford peers when he got that fellowship and she didn't. The other fellows liked her; she liked them.

She even amused folks back in Arkansas with a celebrity story: after a Nicole Krauss event at which the novelist discussed, among many other things, the children she had with the even-more-famous Jonathan Safran Foer, P was waiting for Mat in the hallway outside the reception. Nikhil was tumbling about her feet, getting hot in his parka; P was making Saro laugh by pulling her stroller back slowly then zooming it forward, thinking *cab or subway, cab or subway*, when two matrons huffed up the stairs in wool coats and cloches and inquired where the bathroom was. P gave them directions, but, before they went, one leaned over Nik and Saro, baring pointy teeth, and asked, "And these are Nicole and Jonathan's children, I presume?"

"No," P blustered, unable to defend herself on her own professional record because of course these ladies had never heard of her. "They're *my* kids." Just like any other brown woman who got mistaken for the nanny, except, in this case, nanny for a taller, younger, prettier, and more famous writer.

Of course, this could also have happened if she *had* gotten the fellowship. But she didn't—Mat did. And he'd never be mistaken for the nanny.

Did it make it worse that the Cullman fellowship's value was discounted in his mind by his unexpected suffering? He spent that year prostrated by loneliness, exhausted by being podded up with a bunch of neurotic, if likeable, overachievers. He would never *say* P had it better, happily suffocated under kids and parents back in Arkansas, because that would be ridiculous, not to mention unkind, but she certainly was not lonely. And she got some writing done.

Also, he really liked Arkansas. He liked having a big house and a yard and animals. (So many animals; they came, they went; reptiles, rats, rabbits.) He liked the bike trails, the hiking trails. He liked their friends. She liked their friends, too. And though she had never wanted a big house or a yard (she really, actively did not want a yard), she liked being able to keep her parents well and keep them near. But when she asked what he had liked most about living in New York City, he'd had to think, and then said, "Cycling in Central Park on Sundays. They close the roads to cars."

Not the historic bars, not the unexpected marvels of street life, peoplenoise and hurryburry, not the theaters cinemas art museums architecture neighborhoods. Not even the food.

Cycling in the park. She sank her face in her hands. No wonder he couldn't understand what she had relinquished by leaving Montreal. *If you are ever bored or blue, stand on the street corner for half an hour,* says Maira Kalman in *The Principles of Uncertainty,* speaking of New York, but this had always worked for P in

Montreal, where walking around her block was as refreshing an escape as a novel. If P stood on her street corner in Fayetteville for half an hour, she would see max three people out walking their dogs, two of whom she knew. Everyone else would be in cars.

Mat never said the Cullman wasn't worth it, but he said he would never want to repeat the experience. And now she was applying for that fellowship and others, for a new novel, about an Indo-Canadian government employee writing a novel about a Carthusian monk writing a novel about Marguerite de Navarre. The Canadian was writing during the SARS epidemic and the monk during the Spanish flu, and P was doing original translations of bits from *The Heptameron*. Mat was so excited about it that he was sure everyone would be; despite P's annual failures on the fellowship front, he was positive that she was on the verge of success, and, whether triggered by the return of his New York insecurity or worn and torn by those years nursing Lon and the grief that followed, a dark veil just starting to lift, he was assailed by the prospect of separation.

Which is perhaps why he said to her, as she made her applications this year, "I hope you don't get one."

♦

No, he didn't.

Oh, yes, he did.

But he must have walked it back?

No, he doubled down! "I know you think you need this," he said, "but I learned I don't want to go through that ever again."

This was why you should never think of your husband as your best friend: you needed things from him that you would never ask a friend, and you needed friends for when he let you down.

Throughout that winter, they fought. Not all the time, just off and on. First, they fought some more about the fellowship applications. How would they work it out, he asked, think about it: she would take the kids and he'd be left behind. He was probably right in theory, she said, but she wasn't going to get a fellowship, she wasn't good enough, that was obvious. She was so, he said, her time was coming. Whatever, she said, the real problem wasn't whether she got it, it was that he was undermining her and that he couldn't see how sexist the asymmetry was: he'd had his chance, why shouldn't she have hers? Because he'd been through it, he said, he'd learned, why couldn't she see that?

Meantime, his promotion was advancing through the paperwork maze at whose still center it would surely be approved, and then he'd only have to teach half-time. That's what a Distinguished Professorship got you: the same salary for half as much teaching. On the remote chance that she did receive a fellowship, he could come along for at least half the year. But it was like he couldn't accept or admit it was coming down the pike. Maybe because it didn't fit with his self-image? Maybe because they'd still have to spend a semester apart? Either way, it didn't budge his emotional calculations.

So they fought about this, off and on and off and on, and then, when it didn't go anywhere, they fought about other things. She started fights because she was hung on the cross of the constant tidying and cleaning, food shopping and meal planning. He fought back because he repaired the broken door and the broken chair; he changed the air filters; he updated all of their software— things she didn't value or take account of. And he didn't care if she cooked or cleaned and he never asked her to: he'd rather they live in a dirty house; he'd rather make himself a sandwich. And what about the kids? she'd say, what about hot meals?

Fuck hot meals, he'd say, I love your cooking, but I did fine without it before, so if you want hot meals, fine, but that's on you. It's you.

But. In between. Life.

Halloween: the adults went to the neighbors' annual party as candidates in the Democratic primaries, with Saro as a handler and Nik a secret service agent. Nik, at fourteen, hulked convincingly over his Indian adults in a black suit; Saro, eleven, adopted an air of chic superiority that came a little too naturally.

Thanksgiving: they hosted, as always, a few foreign students assigned to them through a campus service, along with a friend, an Iranian American poet and translator, Mehrzad. He often spent the holidays with them and had always come alone but seemed more so now: though he'd moved to Arkansas with a girlfriend, she'd left him almost immediately for a man she met in church, a very Arkansas story.

After a few solo years, though, he married, in Iran, his parents' neighbor, Minsha, who had known since she was a teenager that they were meant to be together but had to wait for him to get with the program. He was a US citizen and got the paperwork started when he returned that fall for grad school. That was 2014. Minsha was a scientist, which is apparently the worst category of professional to try to import from a hostile nation. Finally in fall 2016, the visa came through. She would come in the new year. P started planning a party. Then came the election, and then the executive orders. Minsha was mired. Her visa expired. They started the process again.

P and Mat saw Mehrzad droop a little further with each passing year, but their holiday dinners, raucous with bickering kids and wandering parents and foraging animals, seemed to revive him. It reminded him of home, he said. "You know how there are so many American novels and plays about Thanksgiving? It's because that's when Americans get together, have fights, make drama. We don't have that, in Iran."

"Exactly!" said P.

He popped another cork. "In Iran, families get together and fight all the time!"

"Cheers to that," P said, raising her glass with one hand and, with her other, trying to hand her dirty plate to a kid who pretended not to see it.

Christmas and New Year's: P's sister and her fiancé visited from Montreal. Christmas was jolly: eating, drinking, reading, opening presents, and walking with cocoa amid the lights at the town square.

For New Year's, they had a party. P's mother made bhel puri, fussing up a mini-buffet of crunchy and savory and spicy components to be assembled in bowls and doused with sauces, tamarind and cilantro. P and Saro made vegan meringues; P and Nik made shortbread cookies; Mat put out a vast vegetarian charcuterie board of cornichons and cheese wedges, olives and nuts. P thought it looked strategic, like resources in Settlers of Catan, but maybe it was just that she saw everything as a battle these days. Shake it off. Prosecco in ice buckets, they reinforced the bookcases and rolled up the rug.

At first, it was just kids on the dance floor, doing their terrible mockeries of disco dancing to ABBA and the Bee Gees. P intervened to show them how it was really done, back in the day. When she was small, her parents and their Indian friends had had disco parties and always included the kids. These were P's only purely joyful memories of her alienated childhood, and one of the things she most wanted to give her kids. Nik and Saro turned out to be better adjusted, yet still loved their parties. Go figure.

Eventually, P's dad requested some bhangra and got on the floor with Saro, Saro's best friend, P, P's sister, the sister's fiancé (an unexpectedly excellent dancer, as Ukrainian Canadians often were), and their director friend Chana, who had taken bhangra lessons back in New York City before moving to Fayetteville. And then, suddenly and all at once, it was everyone. At some point, Mat put on Talking Heads and did David Byrne with an actor friend, Jeff, with whom he'd thrift-shopped that day for seventies outfits. At some point, Ximena and her husband put on Cuban music and were given a run for their salsa money by the neighbors, a white Arkansan and his Chinese-Filipina wife whose kids formed a ring around them while they sashayed about, oblivious. At some point, P's father did a Blues Brothers routine with Gal and Gal's wife. (How did Gal's wife know the Blues Brothers so well? How did P's dad?) At some point, Jeff, Chana, and the rest of the theater folk were inspired to a *Fiddler on the Roof* reenactment and sing-along that ended with a spurious Russian folk dance. (P's sister's fiancé actually knew what he was doing, but no one else could tell.) At some point, the drummers from P's African dance troupe all fetched drums from their cars for an impromptu concert. At midnight, the fireworks went off downtown.

And now it was 2020.

The last weekend of winter break, they went with three other families to a cabin a couple of hours away. P braced herself for the beauty of the Ozarks—it always still took her unawares.

In spring, trees in Fayetteville burst into bloom, tulip trees draped in pink, redbuds in non-eponymous lilac, even the damn invasive Bradford pears showing out in billowy white. In fall, the landscape burst with equal drama into fall colors, scarlets and terra-cottas limned with lime and apricot. Summers were wisteria and honeysuckle, the peonies and lilacs of P's northern youth together with irises and lilies and delicate native flowers she'd never heard of: poppy mallow, coneflower, butterfly weed.

Winter was mostly gray, except for jade-dark vines and pooling trickles of lichen on the rocks' crevasses, not to mention the brightening effect of not having to worry about Arkansas's eight tick-borne diseases. The dearth of foliage, though, revealed what was most arresting in the landscape: the rocks.

Boulders, often twenty feet tall, were strewn magnificently through every wild area in the region, sometimes cracked as though they'd been tossed, sometimes rolled intact up against each other. The Buffalo River was edged by great white bluffs. Hikes would take them along shelves of slate, caves and ledges. In their own backyard, tons—literally—of brown-gray native stone had erupted from the earth when they built P's parents' apartment. Ten years later, they were still using it to build walls and garden beds. The rock: eternal, monumental, it provoked in her the most intimate and spiritual sense of the earth she'd ever had, and in this way, disrupted her thinking about this place and her longing to leave it. The rocks, their friends, her chartreuse study: Things She'd Miss About Arkansas, if ever she got away.

That weekend, with their friends, they hiked forest trails, coming unannounced upon three different waterfalls, incidental magic. In the evenings, P and Mat played Scrabble while the kids were in the hot tub, got in the hot tub while the kids played pool, played pool while the kids played tag. After supper, everyone played Werewolf together. The kids slept in the basement, three rooms with bunk beds and trundle beds and pullouts, giving adults privacy, in the stories above, for leisurely sex.

Or that's how Mat and P figured it.

"How can you not like Arkansas?" Mat asked her plaintively the second night. It was annoying how fun and handsome he was, what a generous lover, how wonderful to be with when they weren't fighting. Plus, even when they fought, she was always aware on some level that there was a fifty-fifty chance he was right. It was a good marriage, even a great one, but that didn't mean she had to keep it.

But he had asked about Arkansas. She began slowly. "You remember, when we first moved here, how surprised I was that I liked it. I did like it, the hippie culture, and it was so easy to make friends. And finding out there was a West African dance group! In Arkansas of all places. It was cool. It defied expectations."

"Like having snakes." Mat had a habit of catching benign local snakes and popping them into one of several terrariums in their living room. Sometimes, they'd winter over before returning whence they came. "You love complaining about the snakes."

"Everyone needs a hobby. Yours is collecting, mine is complaining." She lay down, nestled into him. "Anyway, I didn't let myself believe we were staying. I held back, and held back. Until I fell in love with the stone." She felt his attention perk, enough so that she almost didn't want to go on, give him a wedge. "About eight years in?" She propped herself on her elbow. "I told you that."

He turned to face her, a hand on her hip. "I don't think I knew what a big deal it was."

"I'd always been so attached to the idea of history as human. I'd only ever seen beauty in water or sky, never *stone*. It made me think, *This place could change how I see*. Briefly, I wondered, *Could I stay? Could I be happy here?*" That moment seemed so distant now, so fleeting. "It didn't last. That was the first year we finally managed to go back and spend a summer in Montreal. Which I'd wanted to do since we moved here," she pointed out unnecessarily. He knew.

"I know, I know," he said running a finger up and down her arm.

"I felt at home there the way I never do here. Then forty-five was elected, and . . . you really want to hear all this?"

He shrugged. "No. But I asked."

"All the Confederate flags we drove past on the way to this wonderful house, this retreat." Mat was quiet. "You all fooled yourselves that more progress had been made than actually had." His quiet made her talk more, trying to get a response. "It's not like I'm one of these American liberals who's blind to Canada's problems. Obviously: I spent my first thirty years fighting social justice problems there. Arkansas's just not my place."

He angled his eyes up at her. "You started fighting the day you were born?"

She socked him in the shoulder. "May as well have." He flopped back, playing dead. "No time to waste."

In late February, the fellowship rejections started arriving as they did every year. She would leave the letters on Mat's desk, or forward the emails to him without comment. She had nothing left to say about it.

She recalled serving on the jury for the Canada Book Award a couple of years earlier. There were three jurors originally scheduled—a white woman from Halifax, a white man from Toronto, and P—but then the woman, at the last minute, found a conflict of interest she had somehow missed earlier, and they substituted her with a white man, perhaps the only writer from her region willing to read 220 books in ten days. Good for him.

In the early part of the meeting, P asked a question about criteria. "Like, do we consider equity or balance in the list, at all? Gender, race?"

"No!"

"No."

Both men were emphatically in agreement that the only criterion was best book.

Which was fine with her, though she could have gone either way. They proceeded. Each juror had been asked to submit a top-ten list a few days in advance of the meeting. On receiving the others' longlists, P had read all of their selections, even the ones that were crap.

"Why?" the writer from Toronto asked her, appalled.

"Because I thought they were important to you!" she responded, equally appalled.

He obviously hadn't read theirs. P had had a terrible time narrowing down, whereas it turned out that he'd only liked about three books in the entire 220, yet put books in his top-ten that he didn't even care about, "just to fill out the list."

She'd read a novel he wrote, back when it came out; she'd liked it, but now wished she hadn't.

The last-minute sub was more thoughtful, and terribly underslept as a result.

Finally, they arrived at a shortlist of five books, though it was really down to two: one by an Asian Canadian man about the Japanese occupation of Hong Kong, the other by a white Atlantic Canadian man. Which was to be the winner?

P was uncertain, whereas both men thought the answer was clear: the Maritimer's. "Why?" she asked them.

"It's so relatable," said Toronto, as though that were self-evident. The novel was about a drug addict who may or may not have killed his girlfriend by throwing a teapot at her head.

P looked at their third fellow jurist, who was nodding in great affirmative spirit. "Exactly," he said. "I so identified—the rage, the mistakes."

P had rage. She'd made mistakes. But hers were not in this book.

"I don't relate," she told them, flushing. "I love this novel but I don't identify with any of it. Plus the other book treats a historical episode hardly represented in Anglophone literature. You have to come up with something better if you want me to side with you."

So uncomfortable, being in the minority, especially for a minority. As was clear during their deliberations, Toronto had little trouble dissenting, and didn't try too hard to defend his reasons. Now he shrugged, stumped. Hadn't it occurred to him that anyone in the room might not feel as he did?

Their co-jurist, frowning and considering, offered a way through: the Maritimer's novel was more formally daring. The other was beautifully done and dramatic, but not risky in the same way. He was right and she assented, grateful. It was the right choice.

All this came back to her now, as she thought about committees adjudicating her own proposals and the unlikelihood of jury members who would find the voice or story *relatable* (oh, how she hated that word, she always had, but from a grown man? And a writer?), let alone important enough to fund.

By the first week of March, only one rejection had yet to arrive.

Both Mat and P had applied for two fellowships offered by the University of Arkansas to the Sorbonne. A full year, no teaching duties. They were perfect for it, and they'd heard it got fewer than ten applications annually so you would think their chances were good, but they'd both been turned down several years running now.

In the first week of March, they got the letters in their university email inboxes at the same moment. They forwarded them to each other.

This year, though, P's was different, different from Mat's, and from all the years past, and from all the other letters she'd gotten that year.

P's began, *I am pleased to inform you . . .*

✦

What would they do? What on earth would they do?

Before his Cullman year, Mat's attitude had always been that they had to apply for any and all possible fellowships, that such choices were the best kind of problem. A person should be so lucky.

Now here they were: so lucky. They popped a cork that night. So lucky: they popped corks so much and so often that their dog recognized the sound, jumped at the pop and chased the cork down to chew it to bits on the rug.

P reminded Mat that his Distinguished Professor promotion had been approved at all but the highest levels; it was virtually guaranteed. He would for sure get one semester with them. But either he still couldn't get his head around it or one semester was insufficient, to his way of thinking. After dinner that night, they were sitting in the living room with laptops open, in their own administrative universes, when Mat said to her, "I've decided I want to do whatever it takes to come with you guys."

They had touched on this in prior conversations, but taking a semester off in addition to the one granted by his promotion would be the equivalent of taking an entire year without pay.

"You mean, go into massive debt?" P asked, disoriented.

"Yeah." His face had a strange sheen. "Whatever it takes."

P must have been reveling a little; she hadn't noticed but now felt a glow fading. "I would think that's something we decide together," she mumbled.

It wasn't just a match to tinder. More like tripping on a duff-pile about to self-ignite.

He rose in fury and pain. She reminded him of the things he had done, the things he had said: his own year away, his wish for her failure.

"No," he said. "You did this."

"I did what? What did I do?"

"Why can't you ever apologize? Just apologize! You're so bad at saying sorry."

P's parents had been hanging around after dinner but melted away at the first hint of conflict. The children tried, unsuccessfully, to say good night.

Once they left, P gathered her things and went to sleep in her study.

♥

Her jewel box of a study. On the third floor, chartreuse walls and shelves, an oak floor and faux deco lamp. A red chaise longue, where she lay now, fuming. *Apologize for what?*

It was impossible to be up there and not be reminded of Mat's

kindness and commitment: he saw, when they were house-shop-
ping, that this house not only had space for her parents but an
unfinished attic. "It will be a study for you!" he said. Within
months, he'd had it built, her refuge.

A room like an emanation of her mind. A room she'd never
want to leave behind.

He himself built her desk, the front edge curved like a feather,
the other set against a window looking out on trees, roofs, mountains, sky. When she arose and went to work there in the dark of
morning, she often saw the moon.

Now she lay up there in the dark of night. *Apologize for what?*
For getting a fellowship he wanted? Apologize for being ambitious.
Apologize for putting career ahead of marriage.

Ambitious women were always punished: with loneliness,
with death, suicide or syphilis or painful attrition. It's why
women artists are always asked, in interviews, how they balance
work and family. (Men aren't asked because women balance it for
them.) Women artists are asked because they are still novelties:
it used to be you chose—work or family? But family wasn't her
problem. She could manage the kids and her parents. Her problem was marriage.

The chaise longue was firm and red beneath her, she thought,
a line that had come into her head that morning as she'd floun-
dered to find the next beat in her novel, a hilariously terrible line.
It had given her private amusement all day but she was beyond
smirks now.

To the right of her desk was a low little door to a storage closet.
Now the door creaked and P sat up with a gasp. The cat emerged,
hopped up onto P, and started massaging her shinbone, purring
loudly.

P lay back, thankful to have her mood destroyed, unless she

had just exhausted herself? Her eyelids grew heavy, but instead of sleep, she realized she was returning in memory to another lonely night, another closet, another marriage.

♦

P had backed into marriage—or been backed into it—both times. She had married Mat not merely because she was madly in love with him and he wanted to have babies with her, but because, without marriage, there was no immigration. She would have stayed with him without marriage, but she couldn't.

And previously: she married Hamish because they were living together and her parents were ashamed and afraid of what relatives would say if they found out.

At twenty-five, when she met Hamish, she was almost pitifully naive and inexperienced, easily intimidated by the rich, subtle scent and hush of the menswear store where he worked in Westmount, Montreal's posh Anglo enclave. Walking past one day, remembering her father's birthday was coming up, she had gone in with the vague idea of getting him a tie but balked when she realized the least expensive was five times what she could afford. The only things in her range were some discount-bin no-show socks, which she felt shy even browsing and which didn't seem like her dad's thing. She had a brief interaction with Hamish and might have forgotten it except that, a half-hour later, they ended up in line at the same falafel stand, which she certainly would have forgotten if she hadn't realized, on placing her order, that she'd lost her wallet. Hamish overheard and offered to pay. It was kind but also made her nervous in ways she thought mainly had to do with her, unless she was getting a vibe from him? He was good-looking, or, at least, well-groomed. She refused in a sweaty fluster and spent the next hour going back to anyplace she had taken out her wallet. She avoided Hamish's store, obviously: she hadn't bought anything there.

Ultimately, she figured she must have dropped it down a sewer grating: it was never returned to her, but the credit cards were never used, either. Fortunately, her metro card was in her pocket; she got home and spent the next week replacing her driver's license, health care card, bank cards, library card. She'd lost maybe thirty dollars in cash, but it could have been far worse.

And maybe she even gained, on balance, because a week or two later she ran into Hamish at her local grocery store. She loved that store: disorganized, undercuttingly priced, no decor whatsoever. Practically no one came there who wasn't from the neighborhood, but Hamish said he came there often. He had friends who lived nearby. She recognized him but was surprised when he asked: "Did you ever find your wallet?"

"No!" she said. Thoughtful of him to remember. They walked out together. A few weeks after that, they spotted each other at a street-corner concert. He was the best-dressed man in the crowd, in a copper merino wool pullover and some kind of cravat. Perfect hair and keen, interested eyes. So what if his chin was a bit weak, his hips a tad wide. They toasted each other with street beers and, by the time the night was done, had learned they both had plans to go to the same Me, Mom and Morgentaler gig the following week, and agreed to find each other there.

And then they were dating, not so much exclusively as that neither of them happened to be seeing anyone else anyway.

He'd grown up in, or adjacent to, Montreal, the youngest of three, and had three-quarters of a psych degree from Concordia. What he really wanted to do, though, was to own his own store, maybe even design someday. She identified: she'd come out from Alberta to Montreal for a PhD, but found herself struggling to finish her dissertation. What seemed like depression or ennui turned out to be a different calling and by the time she met Hamish, she was writing and translating fiction, teaching ESL to pay the rent.

Around this time, P's roommate moved west to tree-plant and P relocated into a sunny third-floor studio across from the old garment factories on Casgrain. She hadn't ever lived alone before and was delighting in it. Hamish was on the converse trajectory: his building had just been sold and he and his roommates put on six months notice because the new owner wanted their flat for his mother. Hamish was livid, railing about Montreal's tenant laws and his victimhood, so P never voiced her private feelings: Montreal's laws were the most favorable in the country toward tenants, and it hardly seemed wrong for someone buying a building to have the option to house his family in it. In Montreal, you could pretty much *only* evict a tenant to occupy their apartment yourself or install a close relative, whereas in most North American cities, owners called the shots. But she could see where Hamish was coming from.

Now he either had to find a new place or move back in with his parents in the suburbs. As the months ticked down, he somehow never found a new place—his work schedule, problems with roommates. His parents agreed to let him store some things at their house. On moving weekend, he slept at P's, as he had taken to doing most weekends, and as he continued to, more and more. A year later, they officially moved into what was called a four and a half—a large, sunny double room; two big closets; a closed kitchen; a dining room with a window facing onto a yard—and he fetched the things he had stored in Laval. That month, P, unable any longer to stand her parents' mortification—working uncertain, low-level jobs despite her PhD, and now cohabitation—proposed.

She was in love with him, of course. She could see his flaws or blind spots—his impatient, slightly outsized sense of his own authority, especially on his passions (fashion, jazz, French New Wave film); his erratic money sense; his equally erratic participation in cooking and housekeeping. She accepted them. It was the companionship that hooked her—sharing a home, ready company for a movie or a gig, Saturday breakfast with Saturday papers, always someone to laugh or get indignant at her stories. And he believed fervently in her writing, was positive she was going to make a big splash. He was her loudest cheerleader.

She accepted that every relationship demands compromises. Even the sex, though that was the hardest. He had so many requirements. She was game, but it took a lot of effort, so attempts were infrequent. When she voiced dissatisfaction with this, his response was cold, the opposite of what she hoped for.

"It doesn't matter that much, though, right?" he said one time, being more conciliatory, but it was the kind of question where yes and no could mean the same thing.

When she talked about it with a girlfriend, the friend asked if P thought he was gay. "It would make sense, right? It might even be an advantage in his work." They both laughed. But P had seen no evidence that way. She was willing to go through his elaborate rigmaroles, but couldn't figure out how to get him to reciprocate, given that what she wanted seemed relatively straightforward and yet at the same time vague, open-ended, inarticulable: she wanted a partner to play and explore with. She didn't know yet that she could put it that way (she'd had bad luck with lovers; her desires had never really come up). She wouldn't know until she met Mat.

She recalled all that now, lying in her study, *the chaise longue firm and red beneath her* (ha ha): the relief, the sheer delight of sex with Mat. His sweetness and openness: *What do you want me to do? Does that feel good?* Nothing was off the table. Sex as a fluid-solid-dynamic part of intimacy, not a separate endeavor.

Anyway, it wasn't the sex problems that destroyed her marriage to Hamish. There's no telling how long she might have stayed if she hadn't discovered his big secret.

The year he turned thirty, she planned a surprise party. For her thirtieth, the year prior, he had taken her out for a fancy dinner, so she told him she was doing the same for him. That night, she'd make an excuse for them to drop by a friend's place en route to the restaurant. All their friends would be there.

The stakes felt high. She'd just received her first big grant—ten thousand from the Canada Council for the Arts toward her first novel—and had said in the application that she would spend six months in India. Hamish obviously couldn't come with her. They had fought: "Why get married if you're just going to leave me?" he asked. "You've been to India so many times. Just go for two weeks, even three. It'll be plenty."

But a three-week trip would cost about two thousand dollars; it would cost her only two thousand more to stay six additional months. Life was cheap there and her relatives would put her up; she would return with enough money for four more months in Montreal before she had to start teaching again. Ten months of full-time writing versus five. How could she give that up? How could he ask her to?

Plus she doubted she could do the research she needed in just a few weeks. She wanted leisure to dig around, hang around, eavesdrop—to discover, through the writing, what she needed to know. Her grandmother's cousin had invited her to live in his house in the village for a few months; an aunt had asked her to come on a pilgrimage to a legendary temple. Did Hamish not see the appeal or was he jealous or was he worried she wouldn't come back? "Wait until we can go together," he said, but when would that ever happen? He didn't make enough to take more than a couple of weeks off in summer. She needed to get her book written.

She thought if she could just make him feel secure, appreciated, he would soften.

She got to work planning the party. She wanted some kind of display and asked his mother Mavourneen about baby photos. "I gave them to Hamish after your wedding," she told P, "when I cleaned out the basement. Probably in a shoebox? There's a baby album and some wee shoes and maybe a pacifier."

It was one of Hamish's late evenings at the store. P went into the back of their closet, where she knew he had stashed some things. There were multiple shoeboxes, but they all contained dress shoes, including several she didn't think she'd ever seen, oxfords in a preternaturally soft pink leather and another pair in a style she didn't even know the name of. Pushing aside some suits in plastic, fingering the soft wool, she spotted a battered file box in the back corner. Lifting the lid revealed some hanging files and a shoebox within. She took the shoebox out into the light: baby album, shoes, a tiny, itchy-looking cardigan with a duck appliquéd on the pocket. She flipped through the album—promising, but it stopped when he was five. She remembered, from Mavourneen's slideshow at the wedding, some cute elementary school pictures, and funny ones from Hamish's teen years. It was cramped and stuffy in the closet, so she dragged the box out through the narrow parting in the sea of their belongings, and sat on the hall floor. The hanging folders were buckled, their hooks not resting on the box's top edge. Feeling at the bottom of the box, she found another slim album. There was young Hamish, in the Duran Duran hair of 1988.

She figured she would stash the albums in her dresser until the party but when she replaced the shoebox, she saw that the file folders were still not hanging straight. She might have thought they were just permanently crimped, but their hooks still were not resting on the box's top edge. She felt underneath them; the files' bottoms went all the way down. It was as though the box was too shallow. How odd. From the outside, it looked to be standard size. She pulled the files out. What had appeared to be the usual flap of cardboard that forms the base of such boxes was in fact a separate rectangle, cut to fit—a false bottom. How odd. She fetched a table knife, pried it up, and cried out in surprise.

When Hamish came home that night, she had them arranged on the coffee table in three rows of three, like a tic-tac-toe: nine wallets, all distinct, hers in the center. She had loved that wallet, a splurge when she turned twenty, birthday money from her parents. Soft leather, dove gray with a surprising chartreuse interior, it had made her happy every time she opened it. The others—a white accordion zip with wildflowers, a burgundy snakeskin, a quilted ikat in ombré blues, five black ones of varying shapes and heft—had little in common beyond clearly being women's, meant to be carried in purses, not pockets. There was also, mysteriously, a scarf. *Mysteriously*, ha. As though the whole thing was not mysterious.

Her friend Marta and Marta's boyfriend Asher flanked her on the sofa, their other friend Nurjehan in the armchair. Nurjehan, who lived on the same block, came with a camera and a tape measure, and photographed the closet, the box, and the wallets, inside and out, before pulling out IDs to note down names and addresses. Marta, who lived about ten minutes southeast by bicycle, brought two kinds of dark chocolate and made tea.

They had started talking it through. Nurjehan had never trusted Hamish; Marta was shocked but she'd always been inclined to give people the benefit of the doubt; Asher was there to listen. When Hamish showed up, though, they closed ranks. Nurjehan later told her his face was sort of priceless, like a sped-up film of emotions, ending in pure fight or flight. But P couldn't bear to look at him.

He made a move toward the coffee table and Nurjehan scooted forward. "If you touch them, I'm dialing 911." She had the phone in hand.

He turned toward P. Marta put a hand on P's knee and told him, "Pack a bag."

Nurjehan stood. "We'll give you five minutes. Get what you need and leave."

"Where am I supposed to go?"

Nurjehan barked out a short laugh. "Men! What makes you think we should answer that question?"

They had, about three years earlier, intervened aggressively to extract Marta from a dehumanizing relationship, and would, three years later, do the same for Nurjehan. Thinking back now, from her study in the future, P could only come up with one close girlfriend of her youth for whom she hadn't done that at some point: rescuing each other from manipulative men, deceitful men, demanding men, abusers.

Nurjehan stayed with Hamish—"like brown on rice," as she later put it—watching him from three feet away as he packed and left in an indignant huff. "The noive," said Asher.

The next day, they talked to the police by phone but there wasn't in fact much to be made of the crimes. P could only press charges on her own behalf, and all he took was a little bit of cash plus the wallet. It was a years-old crime, and a minor one, in legal terms: you couldn't really charge someone with causing inconvenience. Nor could he be charged with being creepy, even though that was his primary offense.

Nurjehan called Hamish at the store and arranged a time when he would move out. P was there to make sure he didn't take anything he shouldn't, but she let Nurjehan, Marta, and Asher do the talking, informing Hamish, for instance, that she would expect his half of the rent on the regular until she said he could stop. They gathered he was living with his folks.

And then she tracked down the women. She knocked on doors, talked to old roommates and then old landlords and then parents. She consulted phone books, old and new, at the McGill library. She could have hired a private detective, but she wasn't willing to invest money, only time and sweat. Emotional sweat, especially. She came to think of the process as a sort of Sophie Calle–like performance narrative, though Sophie Calle was, at that time, still five years away from her seminal works on heartbreak and betrayal.

One of them had ended up in Halifax; they spoke by phone and P mailed her wallet. One was in Ottawa, and P took a train one day to meet her and return the wallet in person. The others were still in Montreal. One was a woman, Jonquil, he'd dated. P had heard him speak disparagingly of her. Jonquil couldn't recall how she and Hamish met but it was not impossible it had been shortly after the wallet was stolen. It never became serious between them: "He's a little, comment dit-on . . . full of himself, no? Je me suis lassée vite de ses opinions, très vite."

One, by coincidence, Élisabeth, was someone she'd befriended in dance class years earlier. Hamish had had such a negative reaction toward her that P distanced herself. He didn't trust her, he said. She seemed too straightforward, he said: fishy. P had been puzzled by Hamish's reaction but he was a salesperson, after all. His instincts were probably better than hers. Now they speculated on whether it was because he feared them finding out, even though there was no reason they would make this connection. They parted with a warm embrace and promises to meet again soon, go dancing.

One said Hamish's picture looked vaguely familiar but wouldn't commit to anything further. She seemed very uncomfortable with what P was doing, as though she maybe feared being asked for something. Two didn't recognize his picture or name. Their wallets, it transpired, were stolen after she and Hamish started living together. And one she never found.

She told them all that she was not pressing charges, and that she was not telling Hamish that. She assured them all that if any of them wanted to pursue charges, she would be available to them. She and Hamish would be divorced soon, so testifying against him would not be any sort of problem.

Four months after all of this, she gave up her apartment and went to India for six months.

Her marriage crumbling had opened a chasm under her. That

first night alone, she had been insomniac, vibrating with indignation. But even as the shock faded, other varieties of distress came at her, waking her with the 3:00 a.m. spins: she had no proper job, no savings, nothing secure. She was so relieved not to be dealing with Hamish's preferences: how could she have subjected herself to them for so long? What had made her think it was worth it just to have a dinner companion, a warm body in her bed? She was clearly better off, and it was excruciating.

She weathered it in India, where she simply didn't tell anyone. Six months after her return, she ran into Mat at that artists' residency.

She didn't really want to trust Mat. But she couldn't deny how he made her feel. Maybe she was vulnerable after nearly a year alone. Maybe she felt so free around him because she had changed. She'd had many examples of upright, honorable men in her life—her father, her uncles, her friends, including some of her girlfriends' partners. Maybe #notallmen were smarmy but she didn't fool herself that her experience or her friends' were unusual. But *how can you ever be sure?* You can't, you can't, you can never be sure . . .

All you can do is be honest about your needs, those needs that only a partner can fulfill, and hope that, this time, you have reposed your trust in someone worthy.

Which perhaps was what Mat had done.

Maybe he was jealous of her for getting a fellowship he wanted. Maybe he resented her ambition and wanted her instead to remain a helpmeet.

Or maybe it was exactly what he had said.

In P's favorite Chekhov, "An Anonymous Story," a dissident goes undercover as a butler to get close to a politician he's supposed to assassinate. Instead, he falls into an infatuation with the politician's son's mistreated mistress. He tries to rescue her from her humiliation but despairs, because of course no one can do that for another person. He's not a man who can hold on to her, and, in his darkest moment (both in Constance Garnett's translation and in others'), the close third-person narration slips helplessly into direct address. The dissident thinks of his love, out in the night, realizes he could be the best husband in the world (he may well be the best husband in the world, for her) and that wouldn't necessarily make her stay.

Don't leave me, my darling . . . he cries in his bed. *I am afraid to be alone.*

✦

P drowsed uneasily all night, pushing the cat to one edge of the narrow chaise longue. Early the next morning, Mat came up with a cup of tea for her, coffee for him. P looked at him suspiciously. "What are you offering: forgiveness or an apology?"

He pursed his lips, looked at the mugs steaming. "Those are the only two choices?"

They cupped the hot drinks and watched the sun rise. She knew what he was trying to say—*we will work it out*—because she wanted to say it to him. But she couldn't guarantee that, and didn't want to be even more of a liar than she already felt herself to be.

✦

PANDEMIC DREAM

Yesterday, I saw Katrina Dodson, another Asian American who works from European languages, in an online event. Katrina held up to the camera Don Mee Choi's pamphlet *Translation is a Mode=Translation is an Anti-neocolonial Mode.*

I come from twoness, says Don Mee Choi. *I speak as a twin...* Like Ester in *The Silence,* a Bergman film about a tragic translator, she says, *I also live inside the mirror, the intensifier, the site of my anti-neocolonial translation. Mirrors may be my very own cubby-hole.*

That night, I dreamed that Katrina and I were on a kind of magic blanket, where, as we struggled to translate each verb, small black dragons would come alive to suffer it, dramatizing its meaning as we soared through air.

The first week of March, the university shut down in the middle of P's class on South Asian fiction. She and Mat cycled home together, side by side on campus, racing on the hill. They were making an effort to be friendly, but sometimes it came easy.

Nikhil's shoes and backpack showed he was home but he wasn't in the living room and neither was his computer. She and Mat looked at each other. They had anticipated it, of course. It was never a question of whether, just when.

She went up and knocked on his door.

"Yeah?"

"What's up, honey?" She subtly tried the knob—locked.

"Just changing."

"Changing?"

"I spilled something on my pants."

They positioned themselves in the kitchen. Nik descended, made small talk. Later, he wouldn't answer when P asked him casually where his computer was, but she saw him take a laundry basket upstairs—when had he ever done that, except on laundry day? Never, that's when. She indicated silently to Mat that Nik was taking the computer out of it, and when Nik headed back upstairs, Mat confirmed what they had feared.

P had recently gotten a terrific Peggy Orenstein book, *Boys and Sex*, to help Mat talk to Nik about sex, porn, consent, and the adolescent male. These were things a boy needed to hear about from his dad, even if Mat's dad obviously never talked about such things with him. Mat had been avoiding it for months, as P's tension grew. That night, he started reading the book.

They waited a couple of days. Mat tightened up the security controls on the kids' computers, which always somehow unraveled over time. They were hoping Nik might notice and come clean, but eventually they simply had to confront him.

Several days of talks followed, crisis management, not enough, but Mat wasn't good at initiating low-key chats on difficult topics, as Orenstein suggested—the idea of winging it on a dog walk nauseated him with nervousness. Scheduled chats, that was his solution: Guy Talk, every Saturday morning. Mat would prep for an hour, then get coffee, ask Nik into his office, and muddle through, week after week.

Sometimes, in the worst fights with Mat, P had convinced herself that single parenting would be easier. Really? How would she have handled this, then? She supposed she would have gotten Nik a therapist. Who? And during a pandemic? Imagine: a sullen, laconic teenage boy starting Cadabra therapy to talk about porn use with a stranger? It would never happen.

P watched them go, week after week.

♦

So many of their friends were struggling with their parents: old folks refusing to wear masks, desperate to hug grandkids, dying in nursing homes or in New York. Lon had passed already, some years back, but shortly after, Mat's mother's third husband died and it became clear she couldn't live on her own, nor could the peripatetic daughter of her first marriage house her, caught up as she was in hopping on and off her own marriage carousel. Thus Mat's mom had moved into Mat and P's spare room.

So now, they were seven: Mat's mom in the house, P's parents on the other side of the driveway, a bedroom for each kid, plus an en suite for P and Mat—if Arkansas afforded them one resource, it was space. P and Mat were, again, so lucky: who knew Fayetteville would turn out to be the perfect place to keep your elders safe and close in the pandemic?

Not that it was easy. Where previously they had hired help to clean Mat's mother's room, do her laundry, take her to the store now and again, now P and Mat had to do all that, as well as helping P's parents with groceries, doctor's appointments, learning how to use Cadabra. With seven of them on the compound and home all the time, they joked that it was as hard to get time alone as it ever was.

But they were all so lucky. A big house, secure incomes. They had customarily been going back to Montreal in the summer—that was part of the deal if they were going to live in Arkansas—but Mat had always wanted a proper garden and now he spearheaded the building of new beds, the planting of vegetables. The first fine Saturday, they all dug and hauled, got dirty and sweaty. The dog ran back and forth for sticks. The cat lolled in the sun. The next week, he and Nik got an outdoor Ping-Pong table. Shortly after that, he and Saro got chickens.

P had always woken early to write, so the kids' breakfast fell to her: Mat was a night owl, not an early riser. *You're up anyway,* he'd say. *It's my* writing *time,* she'd say. Now, with kids in virtual school, breakfast could be later, so he took over. Because of a global pandemic, of all the damn things, she had uninterrupted mornings to write for the first time since having kids. A corona-bonus, one of their friends called it: when an unexpected benefit befalls you thanks to the virus.

Mat's promotion was finalized. P's fellowship was deferred. It was somehow decided without discussion that, if ever the fellowship happened, Mat would either teach online from France for the first semester, or just join them for the second half of the year. Somehow, they now understood that would be fine.

He had long insisted that their conflicts were symptomatic of their being overstretched, but P never saw him turning anything down and if he wasn't, why should she? She hadn't been able to relinquish the feeling that marriage was a trap. Not that Mat was trying to trap her, but, regardless of intention, he was part of the problem. Now she saw, reluctantly, how he was also part of the solution.

It would have been terrible to be alone. In the pandemic, she admitted this, in the dark hours when she used to stew. It would be terrible to be single in the pandemic. Two former students had already gone off the rails. One called Mat at midnight, sobbing, asking for a ride: after a night of socially distanced drinking a few blocks away, she was unable to drive herself home and couldn't think who else to call. Turned out her boyfriend had broken up with her instead of quarantining with her. Another called Mat on another midnight to tell him he had realized he'd acquired the power to tell the future. I mean, maybe he really had?

On May 12, the brilliant translator Frederika Randall died. Not from COVID-19, though she lived in Italy, where the virus was raging, and not by suicide, though she had, years earlier, thrown herself out of a third-story window under ambiguous circumstances. Even in the pandemic, people were still dying of all the other causes. Mat organized a tribute to her in the magazine he edited, participated in an online memorial, railed at himself for not having seen her the last time they were in Rome.

The semester closed. Summer stretched wide and uncommonly still. And P, with all her mornings to write, ground to a halt on her novel. Without a trip to France, how to advance it? She hadn't expected to get the fellowship—she thought she'd pay for a month of travel research on her own coin—but she needed to go to be able to write. She didn't know the French Alps or the royal court of Navarre. How did the air smell? What did the accents remind her of? She didn't know how to write fiction in the absence of sensory inputs and happy accidents: what might she overhear in a café? What document might a friendly archivist slip her under advisement?

But if not her novel, what, then? She sat in her study and stared at the walls, green like the sky before a tornado, which is to say, eerie and gorgeous in equal measure.

Suppose I were to begin by saying that I had fallen in love with a color.
So Maggie Nelson opens her tractatus, *Bluets.*
—in this case, the color blue—as if falling under a spell . . .

Nelson cites a study—*half the adults in the Western world say that blue is their favorite color*—which would explain why *every dozen years or so someone feels compelled to write a book about it.*

I love blue. Who doesn't love blue? Blue is easy to love.

Chartreuse is not easy to love: a hybrid, mongrel color. A color that lives on the border, between yellow and green.

On learning chartreuse is your favorite color, a friend, still in the blush of new-friend infatuation, claps her hands: "I love that you have a signature color and that it's so unusual."

Your problematic sister-in-law, by contrast, the one and only time she visits, wrinkles her nose at the color of your study, a color she calls "yellow."

Makeup artist Pablo Manzoni, on the resurgence of the color's popularity in 1988: *Chartreuse is a miserable color. Nobody looks good in it. Because of the high condensation of green and yellow, it is lethal. I repeat: lethal.*

That same year, Margaret Walsh, associate director of the Color Association of the United States, chimed in more dispassionately, saying that chartreuse was being helped by the popularity of other greens, including mallard, teal, turquoise, and hunter. *Chartreuse is probably the ugliest green of all, but it is riding the green bandwagon.*

You only love chartreuse, in other words, if you can't help it.

Daily, she stared out her window as the bright green leaves of early summer thickened into leaf canopy, eye level from her third-floor study. She had never spent a summer in Arkansas. Who had known this was coming? Someone, surely. The first cases showed up in December 2019. Someone had to have known. Scientists? Visionary writers?

P recalled reading about trees and other forest plants communicating with each other through subterranean fungal networks. It sounded insane, but there was a scientist at the University of British Columbia who had, through long and diligent effort, brought it from the realm of science fiction or flaky mysticism into mainstream scientific thinking. Different tree species donated their resources to each other, both seasonally as needed and also at the end of their lives, giving their carbon to the young and alerting each other when stress was approaching. It was why trees did so poorly in a clear cut: people thought that single species would thrive without competition but it turned out they weren't competing.

Were other species talking to each other when the pandemic began? What might the earth have known that people didn't?

PANDEMIC DREAM

Watched Hamilton last night, then dreamed LMM asked me what I would do if I learned I had only four years to live. "Spend it on Saro," I replied, and then woke up, thinking: That's how little belief I have in my writing?

Why write? When I was in my twenties, I was suicidal, and writing saved me. I tell stories in order to live, sure, but if I was dying anyway, Saro would need me most.

(NB: when I saw this in my diary months later, I didn't see the Hamilton reference and mistook LMM for Lucy Maud Montgomery, the great Canadian authoress who first gave me a notion to write, and who also wrote like she was running out of time.)

Zadie Smith, in *Intimations*, her book of COVID-19 essays: *Why do I write? The honest answer: it's something to do.*

P daydreamed a new project: a meandering river of an essay about the color chartreuse.

❧

In *Bluets*, Maggie Nelson confesses to a fantasy, apparently widely shared among Westerners, of being subsumed into a tribe of blue people. She eventually learns of the Tuareg, famous North African wearers of blue clothing. She speaks in the same breath of Isabelle Eberhardt, who got lost among a mystical Islamic sect who, on the surface, have nothing to do with the Tuareg apart from somehow being the fulfillment of this Euro-American fantasy of disappearing into some other color of people. Nelson blushes to say that she knows her fantasy bears all the marks of an unforgivable exoticism.

Her book *Bluets* is rhapsodically interesting. And yet, for a book about color, it's awfully white.

❧

When I was twenty-two, in London on a working holiday visa, I would postpone the lonely walk to the bus after community center dance classes by combing advert boards for small jobs that looked interesting. Answering those ads led me to assist with inventory for a feminist bookshop, to spend an afternoon moving a Ping-Pong table around on the set of an experimental film, to travel to a studio seeking artists' models.

Perhaps I phoned for the address, perhaps it was on the little paper tab I would have torn from the posting's lower edge. A wooden door at the top of a narrow set of stairs, a dark landing on the third floor. I had been asked to come in a certain window of time, and came toward the end of it, but they seemed surprised at my appearance and no one else was there. Two men: Eastern European, heavyset, one in his forties, who answered the door, the other, fifteen or twenty years older, dismantling light stands and collapsing reflective screens. I told them what I was there for. They looked at each other, then the one with the equipment shrugged while the other told me to take off my clothes. "Okay," I said.

There were no easels, no smell of paint, no art students with charcoal-blackened fingers. The room was dusk-lit, bare. I went behind a screen. I took off my clothes. I came out. They looked me over. "Okay," they said. A moment passed. "Okay, fine." They waved me back to the screen.

I dressed and left.

I was not embarrassed to be seen naked: I had German friends, and had gone to lakes with them. But I knew the men didn't need me to take off my clothes to evaluate my suitability as a model. What happened there? They looked me over—nothing else. All I could think was that they were done for the day and wanted a cheap thrill.

I recently told my husband this story for the first time, twenty-five years after it happened, in the aftermath of discovering that our teenage son was watching porn. He looked like his own pity hurt him. "Wow. You were so innocent. I'm sure there were hidden cameras. Maybe your innocence saved you: you didn't look the type."

I didn't look the type, but not because of my innocence. I was saved by my flat chest and body hair.

Innocence: a popular name of *Houstonia cærulea*, a North American plant with small, blue, four-cleft flowers; also called "bluet."

♦

They went for long family bike rides and walks in Fayetteville, the kind of activities they used to do on holiday elsewhere. The statue of Senator Fulbright on campus was surrounded by schubertii alliums, topped by spiky globes. "They're COVID spores!" said Nikhil. The way they saw was changing. Mat had been working covertly on getting that statue moved; one among that summer's many sad revelations for them had been that the great internationalist had also worked to suppress civil rights. How could they not have known? Black people had known, or Black Arkansans, anyway.

"Why don't you want anyone to know you're working on it?" P asked him.

"I'm not doing it to get credit," he responded testily and she surged with affection. You could leave someone you love; harder to consider leaving someone you *like*.

P still had anger, huge anger: the federal government was letting brown and Black and elderly and uninsured and children starve in food lines and drown alone in the fluid-filled pits of their lungs. The venality, the ignorance. But now her rage skipped over Mat, to head unalloyed toward those who created the power structures and held them in place with their sweaty pink hands. Her anger at Mat fled. She didn't notice it go, but she noticed it was gone.

♦

PANDEMIC DREAM

We are in quarantine in some new city, the seven of us plus maybe others, and somehow Mat is accumulating animals: baby birds he's introducing to the cat; a raccoon and some small narrow racoon-like creature, striped tail but much smaller; they're all sniffing each other and Mat is all excited to introduce them and I'm thinking, isn't this how we got into this problem in the first place?

June 7, 2020. Last night, protests raged . . . no, wait. Raged peacefully? Were waged peacefully? Occurred. Protests occurred around the country and the world as a lot of white people finally agreed to agree, at least in public, that Black people are systematically oppressed, in this country, and Canada, and the UK and France, that they have been—at least since 1619, king in, king out, president in, president out—dying with knees on their necks and bullets in their backs.

June 7, 2020. This morning, the *New York Times* reported that the decapitation of an Iranian teenager, Romina Ashrafi, by her father in her bedroom last month, *has shaken the country and set off a nationwide debate over the rights of women and children and the failure of the country's social, religious and legal systems to protect them.*

June 7, 2020. Last night, Mehrzad and his wife Minsha came for a socially distanced wedding reception under our apple tree, six years after their marriage. They'd gotten her another visa this year, and then COVID-19 happened, with Iran among the hottest of hot spots. Finally, the day before her visa was set to expire again, she got out.

We had waited all these years to throw them a party. Now it was just our family and the two of them, under the apple tree. We arranged gifts on a little table for them—champagne glasses and a cake-cutting set. At their feet was an ice bucket with a sanitized bottle of bubbly; they had, as instructed, brought their dishes, cutlery, and water bottles. We had a larger table, with our own dishes and drinks. They had a quiche and we had a quiche, with sage leaves from our garden sprinkled on a parmesan crust. They had a carrot cake adorned with sage flowers, mint leaves, and blueberries; we had a carrot cake decorated with sage leaves and raspberries.

In parallel universes, separated by a buffer of air, we toasted and drank and scooped quiche and cut cake.

It was leafy and shady under the apple tree. Minsha has been suffering photosensitivity here, getting a rash on her arms whenever she goes out in the sun. She and Mehrzad think it's because she has been forced to cover herself up all these years.

Women must cover their hair, arms and curves in public, said the *New York Times* today, describing Iran, where *women work as lawyers, doctors, pilots, film directors and truck drivers . . . hold 60 percent of university seats and constitute 50 percent of the work force. They can run for office, and they hold seats in the Parliament and cabinet,* and also *need the permission of a male relative to leave the country, ask for a divorce or work outside the home.*

"Even here," Mehrzad said, "the regime has followed you!"

♦

They played Ping-Pong each evening, now with the extra challenge of stepping around Ping-Pong-ball-sized chicken poops. Coronabonus: fresh eggs.

Mehrzad came by for a socially distanced drink and remarked, "In Iran it's common to keep rabbits or chickens as pets. In my case, they never lasted. I'd get up in the morning to find them dead. It wasn't even that a cat got them—it's like they saw it coming and had a heart attack. One time, my parents cooked the chicken. I ate it and then they said, 'You know what you just ate?' I turned vegetarian young. It came to me early."

P's friend Marta, in Montreal, sent them a new mixology book, *Drinking with Chickens*. They made Chartreuse cocktails and drank them out by the coop. P said it was research for her essay.

They quoted, in their poshest accents, a line P found in a *Guardian* article by a writer introduced to Chartreuse by a "louche uncle." (Everyone should have at least one.) To be spoken with "an affected stammer," it was from Evelyn Waugh's *Brideshead Revisited*: "Real g-g-Green Chartreuse, made before the expulsion of the monks. There are five distinct tastes as it trickles over the tongue. It's like swallowing a sp-spectrum."

June 8: My dear, brilliant friend Sneha fell down her front stairs in Bangalore and fractured her skull. She WhatsApped me a Sade-bald selfie. She'd always had a tumble of luxurious waist-length hair that set off her huge eyes, and now her eyes looked more mysterious, her dark eyelids heavier. (That might also be age: I had always wanted deeper-set eyes, and now, at fifty-two, I have them.)

It was horrific that this happened during the pandemic, but she said it was a blessing that her skull fractured; otherwise, her brain would have swelled and the pressure might have done her in. A huge brain like hers? What's in it has to come out. Forcibly contained, its contents could have killed her.

❡

"Probably one of the most private things in the world is an egg, until it's broken."—famous quote from M. F. K. Fisher, which Tamar Adler uses in An Everlasting Meal: Cooking with Economy and Grace, to open her chapter on eggs. Everyone has something to say on the subject of eggs, says Adler.

What Adler herself says: A gently but sincerely cooked egg tells us all we need to know about divinity. It hinges not on the question of how the egg began but how the egg will end. A good egg, cooked deliberately, gives us a glimpse of the greater forces at play.

❡

PANDEMIC DREAM

Everyone got sick of isolating and had a spontaneous dance party on campus, concrete and pillars and seating blocks set into lawns. People shared food; someone played a punk waltz on strings. I picked Saro up and whirled around with her—she was still small. Even the most introverted came—enough! they cried, and helped themselves to sweets, grinning broadly.

But then I realized everyone was forgetting to socially distance, and I started to get very worried. The crowds accumulated, I got more and more anxious. It ended where all the other dreams end, though it started out happy.

❡

P was not particularly interested in the chickens, though they were pettable and comical and chased her as a herd to peck at her toes, suggesting a strong collective nature. When she had the chance, her preference was contemplating Ozark stone.

They had benches in back made of slabs of native stone, built by their friend, a sculptor and mason, who also made their walls, from those stones indigenous to their yard. Mat had taken and placed rocks with unusual shapes or patterns in their herb gardens for variety and interest. And out front, there were a couple of "living rocks," like the cresting backs of sea monsters, humps poking out of the earth from bodies deep within it. How deep? Was that even the right way to think about it? Maybe as soon as it went below ground, it merged into a subterranean network, like a collective identity or hive mind or mycorrhizal network. *Oh, what have we done?*

Sometimes, she'd sit out there with Mat, sometimes with her dad, who said to every passerby, "We're having a drink on the rocks!"

Mostly, though, if people let her, she liked to get tipsy and look at the rocks alone.

♦

PANDEMIC DREAM

I'm at a cottage, with friends, and I have messed something up, so I'm feeling bad, but beyond this is a deeper and worse feeling: I'm on the verge of some decision, about whether to have a boyfriend. In the dream, I'm fifty and have never dated, so chances are that I never will. I never learned how. I am staring down a future in which I live alone for the next forty years, no intimate companionship. It's a desperate feeling—from the root: no hope.

And then I see Mat: he's helping my parents with something on the far side of the cabin, sweet, attentive, helpful. He's handsome, in a loose plaid shirt over a broad chest, looking like the epitome of non-toxic masculinity, stooping slightly to hide how tall he is.

And I think, *Oh, yes. All I have to do is say the word.*

Say the word.

So lucky—the solution to forty years of loneliness: right there.

The deep green garden, its walls plastered with mud and hay, faced the river, with the village behind it. The side by the river had no wall; the river was the border. It was a garden of sour and sweet cherries. In the garden was a house, half village house, half city house, with three rooms and a pool in front that was full of scum and frogs. The area around the pool was paved with pebbles, with a few willows nearby. In the afternoon, the light green reflection of the willows was in a silent battle with the dark green of the pool. This always troubled Mahdokht, for she could not tolerate any conflict. She was a simple woman, and wished that everyone could get along, even the myriad greens of the world.

"Such a tranquil color, but still . . ." she thought.

This is the opening of Shahrnush Parsipur's novella *Women without Men* (in the translation by Kamran Talattof and Jocelyn Sharlet), a novel of Iran set during the 1953 US and UK–led coup.

Mahdokht would sit and watch the conflicts among the water and the willow's reflection, and the blue of the sky, which, in the afternoon, more than at any other time, imposed itself on this gathering of shades of green, and which seemed to Mahdokht to be the divine judge between them.

I don't wish the myriad greens of the world to get along and I reject blue as the divine judge of greens.

♥

If nothing else, writing about chartreuse is an excuse to spend hours looking at the color: Agnes Martin, block; Mark Rothko, lozenge; Joachim Patinir, field; Russel Wright's casual china glaze. Art deco earrings dangling peridots. And rooms, rooms, rooms.

♥

Van Gogh's bedroom in the Yellow House in Arles: painted during a several-day sickness, in which his *eyesight was strangely tired,* or so he writes to his friend Paul Gauguin and his brother Theo. *It amused me enormously to make this bare interior,* he tells Gauguin. *Flat tones but coarse brushwork in thick impasto. Walls in pale lilac, floor in an uneven, faded red, chairs and bed in chrome yellow. Pillows and sheet a very pale lime green, the blanket blood-red, the dressing table orange. Blue washbasin, green window. I wanted to express utter restfulness with all these very different colors.*

The Van Gogh Museum and others echo Van Gogh himself, saying that this small canvas communicates a sense of domestic comfort and restfulness. A piece in *ARTnews* cites one art historian on *the friendliness of the scene, filled with square, solid objects among which Van Gogh was literally at home. The instability of the outside world is gone, and one can imagine the worrying tension of the brows of the* Portrait of the Artist *relaxing in the atmosphere of this refuge,* as well as another who says, *The painting itself constructs a domestic ideal, emphasizing security without claustrophobia, filling coolness with warmth, and implying companionship.*

This is projection and wish fulfillment and worse: taking an artist at his word. What artists intend and what they end up doing are very separate matters, as critics should know. Artists are notoriously blind to their own work, and Van Gogh himself said he was having trouble seeing.

Utter restfulness, un repos absolu: repos can also be translated as *rest*, while *absolu* is encompassing. Total rest: who was Gauguin but a harbinger of Van Gogh's early demise?

He has slanted the walls inward; he has given no view beyond the window, whose panes are also angled into the room, as though he tried and failed to pull them open. No air, no escape: the colors are gentle and compatible, yes, but the painting radiates fever, fervor, shame. *Portrait of the Artist as an Empty Room.* He is meant to be resting, so why isn't he in bed? If his vision is so tired, why is he painting?

The broad lines of the furniture furthermore must express abiding restfulness, he emphasizes in another letter, this one to his brother Theo. *Portraits on the walls, and a mirror and a towel and some clothes. The frame—since there's no white in the picture—will be white. This by way of revenge for the enforced rest I was made to take.*

He only started painting in his late twenties, makes hundreds of paintings, is dead at thirty-seven. He paints like he's running out of time.

In Parsipur's novel, five women will flee to the garden where Mahdokht cowers at the start, the garden with the reflecting pool like a window, the garden that will be a refuge from men—their eyes, their hands, their violence, their rules—and from the city's crowds and bustle. Mahdokht thinks about *smoke and swirling clouds of dust from passing cars and pedestrians, and the sadness of windows in the burning sun.*

"Damn these people," she thinks. *"Why don't they understand that the windows can't cure the pain of this country?"*

All you can see through the window of Van Gogh's room are shades of green: pistachio, avocado, chartreuse. Shutters? Curtains? An abstraction of the light through leaves? Or just pure greens?

Books are sometimes windows, offering views of worlds that may be real or imagined, familiar or strange. These windows are also sliding glass doors, and readers have only to walk through in imagination to become part of whatever world has been created or recreated by the author. When lighting conditions are just right, however, a window can also be a mirror. —RUDINE SIMS BISHOP on how rarely children of color have seen themselves in books until recent times.

Mirrors and photos are the only ways I can see my own face, but, inevitably, what I see is not *how* I see myself. *A painting must depict the act of seeing, not the object seen,* says Patricia Hampl. How does that apply to self-portraits?

In Parsipur's novel, a woman, Farrokhlaqa, kills her husband in a slapstick accident brought on by a strange secret hidden inside her marriage: his affection.

Her husband, who only ever treats her with contempt, watches her surreptitiously through his mirror when he ties his tie, prolonging the small chore because it's the only way, the only time, he can look on her with love.

He didn't want to look at her face to face. Every time he looked her in the face, he could only smile with contempt. He couldn't help it. He didn't know why he felt such loathing whenever he looked at her. In fact, when he was far from her, or could watch her unobserved as he did now, he liked her. More than anything or anyone in the world. But whenever he had to face her, the old hatred welled up in him again . . . He knew that she must not, even for one moment, know how much he desired her.

Then, one day, her image, her double, inspires him to try to do better. "Farrokhlaqa, dear," he dares to say.

She trembled. He had never spoken to her that way. She looked up. There was no derision in his eyes; he was looking at her kindly. Farrokhlaqa was frightened. She was certain that he was planning something. She thought, what if he kills me?

Her instinct is to preemptively punch him in the stomach. Taken off guard, he falls down the stairs and dies.

Unexpectedly a widow, Farrokhlaqa buys the house where Mahdokht has turned herself into a tree to escape forever the predations and standards of men. It is a small house facing out on the garden, presumably designed in the Persian style, around a rectangular pool held by a stone frame, resembling a mirror or window.

Van Gogh made many self-portraits that show his actual face, but I want to touch on two other famous *Portraits of the Artist in Absentia*: *Vincent's Chair* and *Gauguin's Chair*.

Vincent got that chair for his friend, who never occupied it: he came late and left early, because they fought. Then Vincent cut off his own ear.

Look at what the chairs tell you about the men.

Van Gogh: earnest, awkward, reticent, clean lines and plain speech.

Gauguin: showy, evasive, urbane, trailing destruction in his slick, shadowy wake.

A painting must depict the act of seeing: I knew this applied to the painter, but is it possible that a painting also depicts, predicts, evokes, the future viewer's *act of seeing* as well?

Gradually, three other women join Farrokhlaqa at the house. Each has been shaped in relation to men, but what seems both surprising and inevitable are the ways they develop in retreat from them. Mahdokht becomes fully, gloriously arboreal. A pinched, conservative woman ends up marrying her friend's abusively conservative brother, just as she always wanted to. That is to say that each continues to develop more or less as she might have otherwise. So why retreat? Because:

Who would you be, if you opted out of that system? How are you deceiving yourself? Shutting men out might be a relief, but it doesn't make sexism or misogyny go away. Plus men, or that is to say, certain specific men, have their appeal.

Farrokhlaqa tries to write poetry. Every Friday, she throws a party, inviting journalists, poets, painters, writers, photographers, trying to gather to herself a social and intellectual significance that has eluded her. But she is not actually writing, and not becoming famous as anything but a hostess. One Friday, a hundred people arrive and she erupts, *screaming at the gardener like a madwoman. "What am I supposed to do with all these guests?"*

"Don't worry," he says. He is the lone man who lives at the house;

no name, only a title: The Kind Gardener. *"We'll make the tree sing. From now on, don't invite anyone until you've composed poetry. What's the point of them coming and eating all your food when they don't help with anything?"*

He's coaching her to seek significance in her own work, not in social visibility or the sating of others' appetites. She never turns out to be much of a poet, but it's a lesson she needs to learn either way, a value men imbibe early, which is perhaps why it takes a man to teach her.

The gardener went away and the tree started to sing. All over the garden, the guests fell silent. It was as if there was a drop of water seeping down into the ground, and all of the people were within this one drop, which was like an ocean containing them all. The drop that was like an ocean went down to the depths of the earth, where it mingled with the sensation of the soil, millions of particles were the guests in the water and the soil, in a dance that began and would never end . . .

A green illusion began. The earth and the sky were green. Green permeated all the colors of the spectrum. The people scattered in the fog, in which they were absorbed and were finally dropped from the ends of leaves in the form of dew.

After this final epic party, Farrokhlaqa shuts herself away to get on with her damn writing.

♦

Stravinsky's elemental Le Sacre du printemps, *"a biological ballet," according to Jacques Rivière, editor of* La Nouvelle Revue Française, *who, acknowledging in 1913 that Stravinsky wanted to portray the surge of spring, also insightfully observed that the work was "not the usual spring sung by poets, with its breezes, its bird-song, its pale skies and tender greens [but rather] the harsh struggle of growth, the panic terror from the rising of the sap, the fearful regrouping of the cells. Spring seen from* inside, with its violence, its spasms and its fissions. We seem to be watching a drama through a microscope." —ALEXANDER THEROUX, *The Secondary Colors*

♥

The word *paradise* entered English from Persian, our Iranian poet friend Mehrzad told me when I first read Parsipur's novel: its Persian counterpart means simply *garden*, he said, though the *OED* makes it sound more complicated, with references to Xenophon, and to Ecclesiastes and the Song of Songs, in which the Hebrew word *pardês* is understood to mean "the park of the Persian king," and to the Avestan word for an enclosure.

♥

When Erasmus referred to the Garden of Delights, he wasn't talking of Paradise, but of those monasteries founded in the Middle Ages, says Henrik Stangerup in the *The Idea of Blue*, his monograph on the faintly tragic Flemish Renaissance artist Joachim Patinir.

Erasmus, he says, *spoke in exalted terms of "the pleasures of solitary life," and the pure joy of encountering God in that solitude. Erasmus, however, wasn't meant for the monastery.* (I am working from a French version of Stangerup's book. The French translator has not, for some reason, used *monastère* for monastery, but *couvent*—convent, or charterhouse.)

Saint Jerome guided Erasmus as he quit monastic life to become an itinerant humanist and disseminator of that early translator's work, a wanderer. *We could have met these monks under a Patinir sky*, says Stangerup, *on the steep mountain paths, beside the Mnemosyne river . . .*

✦

"What's a charterhouse?" I asked my husband.

"Some kind of a . . . a governmental or administrative building?"

"I thought maybe, like, a building at a seaport where they keep track of what's going in and out. Charters, ledgers, that kind of thing."

"Yeah," he concurred. "Something like that."

It only needed brief investigation to find out how far off we were: *Charterhouse* is nothing but the English phonetic rendering of *Chartreuse*, the name of a mountainous region in France, named for the village Saint-Pierre-de-Chartreuse, formerly called *Caturissium*, *Cantourisa*, *Catorissium*, and *Chatrousse*.

It may have been named for some fighting Gauls, former inhabitants of the region, a tribe called the Caturiges.

Roy Andries de Groot, in *The Auberge of the Flowering Hearth*, his cookbook of this region's cuisine, offers an etymology I don't see anywhere else, saying the name came from Romans who took control of the remote valley and founded the village, which, in their day, consisted only of a few *catursiani*, or huts, formally defined by de Groot as *a little house where one is alone in an isolated and wild place*.

In 1084, Saint Bruno founded his monastic order in this same area: the Carthusians.

But had my husband and I been so wrong in our parsing? Obviously, a monastery is a house, for monks. And what is a charter? A written document, granting rights to land or founding some institution. Saint Bruno and a band of six like-minded monks had been directed to their original location by the bishop of Grenoble, who had had a dream of seven stars hanging over the desert of Chartreuse. (*The word does not mean a desert of sand, without life,* de Groot explains. *This 'desert' is teeming with animals and birds. Its earth is rich with wild fruits and mushrooms. Its fields are lush pastures,* none of which explains the application of this word for this anomalous purpose.) The land was granted by local lords: in 1811, Grenoble's librarian acquired a load of their charters, which had been found at the Grande Chartreuse.

So while in English we call a Carthusian monastery a charterhouse, the French call it a chartreuse, the same word as for the valley, for the color, for the liqueur, a single word that breaks open like a geode, to reveal so many facets. Saying the word—*chartreuse*—is like swallowing a sp-spectrum.

Joachim Patinir painted a large triptych, called *The Penitence of Saint Jerome*. In it, a single shadowed vista of rocks, river, fields and sea coast stretches in bucolic teals, jades, and pigeon's-breast blues across the background of all three panels. In the middle ground are midscale human dramas. In the foreground are three hermit-saints in action: John, baptizing Christ; Jerome, castigating himself; and Anthony, tested by monsters and women. Jerome takes the center, the sky behind him dashed with blood-red from a fleeing sunrise as he kneels before a doll-size Christ stretched on a little crucifix, pulling his peacock-blue robe aside to bare his skinny chest.

Saint Jerome does his shameful business on a chartreuse patch of ground hidden from the world by rocks. All the rest of the receding fields in that central panel are velvety variations on the same soft yellow-green. While the writer Stangerup wants to talk about Patinir's blues, his rocks and rivers, I want to look at *this one green*, invisible to Stangerup, apparently, as with pauses in music or blank spaces on the page.

Jerome and Anthony endured their trials alone. John the Baptist also was a hermit; Patinir just painted his iconic moment, when he happened to need company. And yet they are all in the same landscape, in the same space, the same time. It must be: no natural landscape holds its colors consistently from year to year, or season to season. And in Jerome's panel, one of the middle-range human dramas behind him features Jerome himself, forgiving the thieves who stole his ass.

If all of Jerome's life could happen at once, it makes sense that other saints, too, might go about their lives in that same time and place, yet never cross paths.

♥

Carthusian monks' cells are arranged in a square around the monastery's cloisters. Each cell consists of two rooms. One room has a fireplace and was used as a kitchen until it was decided that the monks' time was not well used in cooking for themselves; in the six hundred years since, they have received their meals through a hutch in the door. The other room contains a narrow bed enclosed in a sort of box, like a train berth, and a dining table for one, set in a window embrasure. Beyond these rooms is an enclosure for solitary recreation in bad weather and a garden to be worked when it is fine outside.

But the focus of all of this thoughtful design is *between* these rooms: *a tiny study whose only furniture consists of a table, a desk and a few shelves holding books of piety which remain there permanently and books of study loaned from the common library*, says The History of the Great Chartreuse, a late-nineteenth century portrait by "A Carthusian," translated into English by one E. Hassid.

In the deep calm of his little retreat, the Carthusian can give himself up to study in the most complete tranquility. Here he enjoys a solitude within a solitude, if one can be alone in the company of the world's great intellects, who speak to us through their works.

The author invokes Thomas à Kempis: *I have sought peace everywhere and found it nowhere, except in a corner with a book.*

Guigo the Carthusian, describing the contents of a cell at the beginning of the twelfth century, remarks that the monk is given books to be kept *with all the care of which one is capable, for books are the imperishable food of the soul.*

The Carthusian is never happier than when in the deepest solitude. *O beata solitudo, O sola beatitudo!*

♦

When I brought Shahrnush Parsipur to the University of Arkansas to read, I asked our friend Mehrzad to introduce her. "Our Shahrazad," he called her, in the first sentence.

As is well known, Shahrazad is the heroine of *The Arabian Nights* tales, subject of a Persian king, Shahriyar, who, on learning his wife cheated on him, not only put her to death but vowed to take a new wife each day and have each put to death the next morning, as insurance against his ever again suffering this particular humiliation.

After three years of this, Shahrazad steps up and volunteers to marry him. Her plan is to save the women of her kingdom. On her wedding night, after sex, her sister, Dunyazad, who had accompanied her to the bridal chamber but stayed discreetly out of the way until now, rolls out from under the bed and says, *Shahrazad, tell us a story to ease the passage of time.*

They call for refreshments—dates, almonds, chickpeas roasted with lemon rind, and sugared rose petals—as Shahrazad thinks of what tale she should tell.

Ah, yes! she says, and commences "The Hunchback's Tale."

When the pink rays of dawn hit the bed frame's gilt edges, King Shahriyar blinks, amazed: he hadn't even noticed the dark hours of the night rolling by, trying to get his attention.

Shahrazad, too, blinks and breaks off her story. They all stretch and yawn; she kisses her new husband's cheek and instructs him to have a good day, and then the women get back in bed.

Wait, he says. *How does the story turn out?*

She's already half asleep. *I'll tell you tonight,* she says. He walks out, dazed, rubbing his eyes, his mind full of the scenes and people of Shahrazad's tale (as though they spent the night riding a magic carpet, his arms wrapped tight around her middle), and runs into the elite cadre of executioners already arrayed outside the door. He doesn't even recognize them at first, in part because he normally doesn't look at them; normally, he just waves them into the chamber as he hurries past, lets them do his shameful business. Now he startles as he meets their eyes. He sees how three years of forced participation in serial-killing-by-proxy has etched lines into their faces, loathing for him and themselves and this whole fucked-up world.

I'm going to let her have one more day, he tells them. *But stay on guard.*

When he says this to them the next morning as well, and then the next, he checks their faces for insolence or derision. Do they disrespect him for not sticking to his resolution? The guards are well trained and don't betray their emotion. They don't know what's going on in that chamber, but they're relieved. It's been horrible: all the young lives wasted, girls like their own daughters. One of the brides was in fact an executioner's daughter; he didn't participate in her arrest, but guillotined himself later that day. Everyone knew it was not merely the loss of his child. It was the full realization of what he was inflicting on all those families, and a whole generation of young women.

What they don't know is that Shahriyar, too, is relieved. His rage petered out after the first months. After that, he stayed the course to keep up appearances. Then he did it because it was what he did. When he thought about his wife—the first wife; he couldn't really think of any of the others as wives, not really, more as concubines, multiple, disposable; a wife is someone you have an intimacy with; you confide in her; you listen to her; you give her your heart—well, he tried not to think about her, which got easier with the passage of time.

And now this new distraction.

Saint Jerome in the desert made Christ's words his own, says Stangerup—*Come with me to a place apart in the desert where you can be alone and rest yourself a little*—who then recalls Claude Lévi-Strauss's words, on *"the brief intervals when our species can bring itself to pause its hive-labour (to contemplate) a rock more beautiful than any of our works."*

The Great Chartreuse has survived multiple fires, avalanches, the plague. What has come closest to destroying it, though, has been the order's two forcible dissolutions by the French state.

The first of these, at the end of the eighteenth century, is described by the Carthusian in his history as *the disappearance from France, after seven hundred years, of the order founded by St. Bruno, which offered a refuge or place of quietude for those spirits who were fearful of the world, or whom it filled with sorrow and distaste. For this inestimable service they should have escaped the general disaster, but it was not to be. All of the Charterhouses fell, and almost all will never rise again from their ruins.*

It's a cri de coeur: *Yet the inclination to solitude is of all ages: our own century, precisely because it is carried away by a vertiginous activity, engenders in more hearts than might be supposed an irresistible desire for calmness of spirit and tranquility of soul. But where is this mysterious joy which attracts them to be found? Formerly, the numerous charterhouses scattered throughout France aroused first the idea and then the love of solitude. Now, since humanity does not change, the desire for solitude remains, but there is no way of satisfying it. Thence the numbers of wretched souls: unfixed, going astray, seeking in ways most dangerous and disastrous to society an unknown happiness that they would have found in the cloister but will never find in the world.*

In *The History of the Great Chartreuse*, the Christian God is not absent, but not nearly so salient as I expected when I opened it with my secular Hindu hackles raised.

Rather, what the monk says again and again is that the Carthusian seeks and finds, in his place of refuge, *leisure*—for solitary reflection, reading, and writing. Several hours of communal prayer daily alleviate the loneliness of silence; good works in the surrounding community, such as the building of schools and hospitals, cure the taint of selfishness. On specific days, at specific times, the monks eat communally and talk together.

This is a strictly regulated Christian—nay, Catholic—community, without doubt. No sex, no kids, no music or movies.

And yet, what does A Carthusian Monk hold up as the value and gift of his life, an orb glowing in the chalice of his hands? Not prayer, not austerity, certainly not self-abnegation.

Rather: the leisure—and pleasure—of being alone with one's thoughts.

♦

As I write this, we are eleven months into the COVID-19 pandemic. I can smell the coming of the Ozarks spring. There are even some yellow blooms in my front garden, something I planted last fall, I'm guessing. We had our first vaccine doses two weeks ago and hope to achieve immunity right around the one-year anniversary of the shutdown. The world has been waiting for this magic bullet, waiting to go back to the way we were: climbing from one rung to the next, changing the climate, zooming around for real instead of virtually. But we already know we can't and won't go back. We have changed permanently. We will emerge already transformed.

The term *magic bullet* was coined by Paul Ehrlich, the Nobel Prize–winning scientist who developed salvarsan, the first effective treatment for syphilis. The term refers to a remedy that has no side effects or collateral damage.

In 1837, the novelist Stendhal came to the valley of the Great Chartreuse, Roy Andries de Groot relates in *The Auberge of the Flowering Hearth*, translating a long excerpt from Stendhal's personal papers. The writer is coming along an alpine path on horseback and joins a jolly party of young married couples but as they descend into the valley, a monk runs out toward them, having heard the women's laughter. Stendhal wrote:

> Apparently, the Chartreuse hermits are horrified by the sight and sounds of women . . . Now one of the hermits came towards us, also looking quite terrified by the sight of six beautiful young women. He said at once that, if they insisted on coming into this valley, they would not be permitted to approach the hermitage but would be lodged in the infirmary some distance away. He added, rather pointedly, that in ancient times women were forbidden to enter the valley. But the revolution had changed all that . . . I admit that at that moment I

thought our entire journey to be a ridiculous mistake . . . Why should these hermits, trying to escape from the world of men, trying to find peace and solitude in this wild place, be disturbed by our curiosity, which was both cruel and indiscreet? Perhaps our coming would revive some intense pain which they sought to forget.

Women without men, men without women.

The monks permit Stendhal and the men to stay at the Great Chartreuse, the women some distance away. They look around.

Our friend the hermit showed me their excellent library. I could see, from the dust on the shelves, that no one ever touched the books. I was sufficiently simple-minded to say: "You should place here some books on botany or agriculture. You could surely grow, in this place, all the useful mountain plants of Scandinavia. Surely such a study would amuse and interest many of you." He drew himself up and said: "But m'sieur, we do not wish to be interested, or amused . . ."

Critic and mythographer Marina Warner has suggested that clever, inventive Shahrazad was the originator of the talking cure. Night after night, she draws Shahriyar through magic mirrors, into dream worlds, stories within stories within stories. They voyage to the corners of the empire—India and China and the interiors of great houses—they see fishermen, genies, princesses, and parrots. There are books of enchantments and books of poisons and poisoned books and enchanted books, books, books, books.

After three years, Shahrazad has borne the king a child and Shahriyar declares his misogynistic campaign officially over: not only have a thousand women been spared, Shahrazad has rescued all womankind.

Throughout, the storyteller and her listeners relax in repose. I picture them on a divan of the sort my family in India used to have, a low bed with multicolored bolsters and a thin mattress so that a tray, perhaps with silver mugs of sherbet or cardamon green tea, could be set safely upon it. I see a diaphanous canopy—wound carelessly around the bed frame in daytime, it is let down at dusk against mosquitoes and excess light.

Freud, ever the Orientalist, filled his study with tchotchkes of the mystical East, particularly *divinities from Egypt, Greece, and India, many of them oracular, scribal, channelers of wisdom, solvers of riddles,* says Warner in *Stranger Magic: Charmed States and the Arabian Nights.* He called his daybed, what we now term "the analytical couch," an ottoman.

Daybeds, says Warner, *suggest a specific form of consciousness, the state of reverie that arises when someone is still awake or rather semi-awake, a receptive state of consciousness—reverie and daydream, rather than dream; subconsciousness rather than unconsciousness (even a hypnagogic condition when mind-pictures are most vivid). These are indeed times open to "l'invitation au voyage," to travel towards "luxe, calme et volupté."*

It's not by coincidence that I have a chaise longue in my study. I often take to it for a midmorning snooze. It reinserts me in the dream-space of fiction. Freud's "couch" was also a chaise longue but Warner takes pains to distinguish it from those to which women were confined in this era, the "rest cure" prescribed to neurasthenics such as Charlotte Perkins Gilman, *whose ferocious parable, "The Yellow Wallpaper" (1892) dramatizes a woman going mad under the constraints of such treatment.*

The daybed is for freedom, *for abandoning oneself, alone or with others.* Freud covered his with an oriental carpet, so that his clients flew upon it through their dreams, back through dark nights of memory, forward into fantasies. *Time is made to curl up end to end so that distance draws near and the past becomes present; depth disappears in a flattening effect that brings up to the surface what once lay buried.*

The daybed, divan, chaise longue, sofa, couch-with-carpet is a stage where stories expand into life and listeners step into them on air. It is a portal to parallel universes, a vehicle to meet former or future or *other* selves.

♦

Tamar Adler's *An Everlasting Meal* is the quintessential pandemic cookbook: a manual, sheathed in poetic and entertaining prose, on how to cook at home but not get bored either with cooking or with what you cook, even when you can't go to the store, even when the store shelves are pocked by supply chain problems. And yet I was not brought to Adler by the pandemic or by cooking at all. Rather, I was brought to her by seeing, in the *OED*, the most obscure definition of chartreuse yet.

In descending order of familiarity, chartreuse is:

-color
-liqueur
-monastery
-remote alpine region and
-*casserole!*

A chartreuse, it turns out, is the name of a molded preparation of cooked vegetables—a cabbage casing supported by a self-congratulatory arrangement of carved and snipped carrots, turnips, and beans—enclosing some bird-game such as pigeon or partridge. It looks garish and sounds grotesque. How on earth could this flashy monstrosity share a name with a band of modest, self-effacing, vegetarian monks?

In a 2016 article, Adler, who had been led from one chartreuse to another by a similarly accidental route, explained: *The common story for the connection between Carthusians and a vegetable construction concealing meat is that the name is literal: that the obedient monks were not so obedient—they hid meat inside cabbage and carrot to hide transgression. But neither my mystically riveted soul nor religious history support it. As Ken Albala, director of food studies at University of the Pacific, wrote me, for most of Christian history, vegetarianism was dangerously close to heresy. Since Augustine, a central assertion of the church was that the earth was made for our use and animals for our table. More likely is that the dignified monks ate their bread and roots and wine, as they vowed—and then some late-18th-century chef made an edible vegetable sculpture with meat at its center and called it chartreuse, a wink at the leguminous monks.*

To mock them, in other words. Fair enough. The only thing worse than someone *acting* holier-than-thou is someone who actually *is*.

This week, I watched *Into Great Silence*, a documentary about the Great Chartreuse with no dialogue, no voice-over, no score. Oh, boy, did my family love it. Even my mother—herself a committed practitioner of a rigorous form of silent meditation—got in on the act.

"Nikhil, sit down, come," she said, as our son slouched past. Onscreen, a lay brother entered a dim barn and fed some cows. "You're missing the most exciting part!"

♦

For this soul needs to be honored with a new dress woven
From green and blue things and arguments that cannot be proven
          —PATRICK KAVANAGH, "Canal Bank Walk"

♦

Patinir, like all Flemish landscape painters, had in his studio crystals that he used as models for his rocky landscapes.

The Danish writer Stangerup had only had two happy times in his life, once in Brazil, once in Mexico, and on both, he says, Patinir accompanied him. *I withdrew from the world for a year to write* Lagoa Santa, *his novel about a Danish naturalist in Brazil. Patinir fed my inspiration, almost writing the book with me. At night, we shared the same dreams, walked together on the banks of his rivers, slept in his huts, compared the flowers of his Flanders with those of my Denmark and those of Minas Gerais. The birdsong was not as he had imagined it. We often met St. Jerome on our walks.*

Patinir himself loved to travel, and found particular inspiration in Provence: *Patinir, the melancholy and febrile bohemian, knew an enchantment much like that found by Van Gogh in the same place. He felt at home. He wanted to mix these landscapes with the memory of the river of his childhood, and with all that is blue.* But Patinir's blue, says Stangerup trippily, as though getting high on Patinir's colors, *is more than a color. It's beyond the visible. It's the blue revealed by Plato, a sublime reality, the idea of blue.*

I have tried, here, to write about chartreuse as the idea of green, *beyond the visible,* an essence, elusive, not anything we need to agree on, despite which, thinking about it at the same time, in this same space, we might be borne toward a brief mutual rapture.

Alexander Theroux in his essay on green, in *The Secondary Colors*: *Alma in Tennessee Williams's* Summer and Smoke *literally finds the meaning of life in "how everything reaches up, how everything seems to be straining for something out of the reach of stone—or human—fingers . . ."*

Stangerup, invoking Claude Lévi-Strauss: *Before "the entire spectrum of human cultures has finally sunk into the abyss dug by our own frenzy," we can still find happiness in the contemplation of one of the rocks alongside the Mnemosyne river.*

Jody Gladding, quoting Robert Smithson: *Words and rocks contain a language that follows a syntax of splits and ruptures. Look at any word long enough and you will see it open up into a series of faults, into a terrain of particles each containing its own void.*

The *New York Times* What to Cook This Week section: five easy recipes, readily adaptable to whatever you have on hand. It's an extension of the *Times* cooking section's credo, *to help home cooks of every level*, but, in the pandemic, when cooks of every level were stuck at home, I imagined us all making the same things at the same time, mixing and pouring, bending and lifting, the bonding effects of synchronous movements, as with my dance class, the closest I've ever gotten to feeling like I'm on a team. Apart from marriage, I suppose.

For New Year's Eve, though, I needed something special, something appropriate to the moment: an adieu to our generation's Worst Year Ever. I would make Tamar Adler's own *updated vegetable chartreuse,* one the Carthusians themselves would be pleased to sup on.

I found one other recent article on the chartreuse. The *New Yorker*'s Bill Buford does an apprenticeship with chef Daniel Boulud, just long enough to make three traditional French dishes, including a chartreuse. *There were obvious challenges in making a chartreuse. For me, there were additional challenges, in knowing how to think about it,* Buford says, inverting the hierarchy of effort. His problem, he says, is the name. Stretching his detective work to fit the three days required to make the dish—still making it look as though he is working harder than everyone else—he finally arrives at the same conclusion that took Tamar Adler a paragraph, except that where she marvels, he jeers: *The dish is, in fact, named after a bunch of monks, mountain freaks who never knew the fatty happiness of a steak frites and a glass of red.*

The old-fashioned chartreuse is gaudy, overdecorated, ugly, in contrast with Adler's colors: undyed linen, wintered-over potatoes, dried sage and grape leaves. Appropriately, Buford's writing is as overelaborate and exclusive as his chartreuse, stuffed with quails, woodcocks, doves, pheasants, and both a pigeon and a partridge never to tweet, cluck, coo, or peck and scratch at the earth again—chartreuse as avian tomb. Bombastic prose, meant for consumption, not participation: if the greatest challenge of *his* chartreuse is figuring out how to think about it, his article suggests he never figured it out, but masked his ongoing befuddlement in empty macho declaratives.

By contrast, because Adler's essential stance on food is not performative but participatory, she not only understands the chartreuse but lets you feel that you arrived at understanding with her in a synchronous sprezzatura movement.

Focusing on simplicity, accessibility, and modesty, Adler reclaims the chartreuse both for its unwitting namesakes and for our times. The chartreuse, she suggests, went out of fashion because we no longer want our vegetables altered into artificial perfection, *boiling them, braising them, sieving them smooth.* These days, *it's the opposite: Our age's cultured eaters want ingredients as nature made them. We want to see the spirit of the cabbage in the cabbage, the mushroom in the mushroom.*

The Carthusians live close to nature and their own souls; their liqueur brings us the spirit of the alpine herbs of their gardens and their mountains; and *a chartreuse,* says Adler, *can serve as the perfect display case for any vision of the natural world, including our own.*

So, to work:

While the new chartreuse, unlike the old, is *not technically difficult,* it is, she warns, a lot of work. Like meditation, it looks easy but demands effort; not the pushing, sweaty kind; the kind that is quiet, disciplined, still and sustained.

Her recipe called for napa cabbage but I wasn't able to get that from our grocery delivery service, so I ordered regular green cabbage, but what came was purple, so that's what I used. From the first, it resisted me. Napa cabbage has thin, wide, flat leaves. Purple cabbage leaves are thick, stiff, and enfolded like brains. Brains don't like to be pried open.

After a half hour of careful work easing the interlocked leaves apart, I had enough that I set to work braising them in a pot of water, salted, per Adler's instructions, *until it tastes like pleasant seawater,* whereupon the leaves' cheerful magenta turned a slightly sinister violet blue.

Even more interesting was the water, which turned a true, bright royal blue. I thought, as I stirred it, of Michel Pastoureau's descriptions of medieval dyers in *Green*, his cultural history of the color, and especially of poor Hans Töllner, licensed to dye wool in blue and black, but discovered to have yellow dyeing vats at his facility. Evidently, Töllner had been dipping cloth in woad *and* weld, making green—a practice strictly forbidden by the Nuremburg authorities. *Legal proceedings were brought against him, over the course of which he defended himself very badly, denied the evidence, claimed that the vats did not belong to him and that he did not understand why they had been transported to his premises.* Should have had Giuliani on his legal team.

Anyway, after four hours of solid labor, I presented my family with an eye-catching "cabbage cake"—my daughter's term for it. It was pretty but more showy than subtle, thanks to the purple leaves, and lopsided. (Like my prose; like me.) It didn't come out in birthday-cake slices but in wobbly slabs that sprawled in relief as soon as they hit the plate. It was also surprisingly rich: relieved by some freshness and crunch from the slaw but squarely in the earthy-umami range, sage and mushroom.

I couldn't eat more than one slice at a time, but with seven at table, little was left anyway, and my second slice was delicious the next morning, topped with a sunny-side egg and supported by a toasted baguette.

♦

Stendhal: *We also discovered, happily, that the Chartreux sell a green liqueur and we all bought a few bottles. It is extremely expensive but very powerful . . .*

♦

Maggie Nelson early in the pandemic, reread Natalia Ginzburg's essay "Winter in the Abruzzi": *that was the best time of my life, and only now, that it's gone forever, do I know it.*

♥

The most famous cocktail made with Green Chartreuse is called the Last Word.

♥

As I brunched on January 1, and thought about Adler's book, *An Everlasting Meal*, constructed around the idea that the remainders of one meal contain the start of another, and about new beginnings, which tend to be built on what went before, I contemplated that extraordinarily beautiful sapphire-blue cabbage cooking water. I couldn't bear simply to toss it, so instead I'd sealed some six ounces in a jam jar. It stayed that color for a day. The day after, it was slightly paler, but not much, and the day after that, it turned a lucid amethyst, by some interior catalysis, as though a genie were in there playing around with metamorphosis, biding her time till release.

P3 Into the Desert

I T M I G H T H A V E been foolhardy to get the instructions in French, P thought as she looked across the town square. But the hotel owner, Avril, hadn't tried to switch into English and who's to say she could have been clearer in a language not her own? She had drawn a map on a piece of scrap paper and enlarged the Google satellite image of the Chartreuse Desert on P's phone to indicate with her finger where the paths threaded along cliffs and through forest.

Nearing the far side of the square, she spotted the sign: Le Mélissard. Ah, it was a restaurant. Avril hadn't said, only that, whatever it was, the trail started behind it. The questions you don't think to ask.

Aakash and Deepa bumbled along behind her, tossing joke insults at each other, paying no attention to their surroundings—the French Prealps, hard not to notice—or to where they were going. It was entirely on her.

Behind Le Mélissard, the trail went both ways. P knew they had to ascend to the left eventually, but it looked as though Avril's squiggle intimated an inclination to the right just at first. They shuffled down a small slope onto the trail.

⋆ * ⋆

P went to her window, drawn by the approaching sound of what could be the largest, loudest ice-cream truck ever, the oompah of some ditty she couldn't quite place. The five llamas who grazed the meadow just below the Hotel Beau-Lieu galloped with urgent purpose to the high far end of their paddock, where they halted cartoonishly and peered toward the curve of the road below. Two emergency vehicles rounded the bend; the first, a yellow van, blared the happy tune P had heard. That's what ambulances sounded like in Saint-Pierre-de-Chartreuse? Would the paramedics, in dirndls and striped caps, exit with stretchers in a cheering gavotte?

As the vehicles disappeared from view, the llamas thundered back to the edge below P's window, in time to see the vehicles mount the slope and disappear into the town behind the hotel.

Galloping back to the other side, they paused on the peak to see another car and a cyclist; back to the near end as they passed; back again for a group of cyclists. P's dog had a similar routine: if he was on one side of the house and saw their car go by, he'd race around the house to greet them on the driveway; if he saw them leave, he'd race around the other way to watch them go.

So: a stage race. The ambulance probably had a more alarming siren setting for accidents. It was yet another detail she couldn't have made up, along with the unicyclist she had seen ascending a mountain slope, along with the way her dinner of cheesy baked crozets smelled herbally of the region's wildflower *alpages*. Not that Nik would believe it. When she left her family in Paris, he'd asked, "If it's fiction, why can't you just write it from imagination?"

She tried to explain: fiction needs a thin lever of reality at least; it can't be conjured out of nothing. He wouldn't be coaxed from his skepticism: surely all the information she needed was online? She'd asked herself the same thing, but said, "Think of the contrast between a Cadabra chat and seeing your friend in person. I can look at pictures and read descriptions but none of that can substitute for the richness of real experience. On a trip like this, the main things I'll learn are things I can't anticipate."

"Like what?"

She looked at him. "*What* did I just say?"

He wasn't convinced, but he didn't really care, either. He was only asking because he and Saro wanted to come along. But P had told them this was a trip she would do alone.

She had wanted to stay at the Auberge of the Flowering Hearth, but it had been hard for her to figure out when to take the trip, and by the time she committed, they were booked up. She visited, though, her first afternoon. The interior looked like it hadn't changed that much since Roy de Groot—a copper-hooded hearth in a flagstone-floored foyer; a dining room out of her youth, with a wood-paneled bar (except real wood, not panels) and red damask tablecloths. What had changed, tragically, was the menu. It was fine, but fixed: a couple of regional specialties, other items you might get anywhere in France. As aperitifs, Bonal and Gentian, stolidly but generically local. No more the rigors and delights of meals bodying forth like genies, apparitions, inspirations from a foraging hike; or a fortuitous chat with a passing sheep farmer; or a bush, tripped upon, in bloom or fruit. In de Groot's time, a printed menu had been impossible: the women who ran the Auberge served you what was available that day, prepared in the best possible way and accompanied by an evanescent variety of liqueurs and wines that, like the food, were flavored by individual flowers and grasses, by a particular day's weather. The meals expressed the mood of the place and passed as moods do.

At home, P had recreated a couple of the items, aware all the while that to do so already violated their spirit and method. Now, leaving the stone courtyard of the auberge, she resolved to smell harder and more subtly the meadows and forest roots, to try to scent the possible undergrowth of disappearing herbs, fungi, maybe whole breeds of animals.

On her six-month in her mother's village twenty years ago, she had been witness to the vestiges of a way of life now largely vanished. The great-aunt she stayed with served a seasonal litany of dishes it would have seemed a violence to export. Tender banana-flower curry, P remembered, and what else? They wouldn't come to mind; they had no place in this landscape.

The auberge vanished behind her as she followed the curve of the road through the mountain's infinite regressions.

Henrik Stangerup: *The birdsong was not as he had imagined it.*

★ ★ ★

Before long, the trail wound left, per Avril's map, and started to ascend. From the forest, it emerged into a sunny meadow, then threaded the flank of a mountain slope. Avril's great-great-grand-father had built the Hotel Beau-Lieu; Avril ran it with her mother. The geography she was explaining to P was in her head, as it had been in the heads of all her forebears, the ancient, dusty footpaths they themselves had worn into the mountains, worn down to stone.

P and the kids came to a fork where the road they were now

walking bent sharply down into the valley. Here, they were meant to go right, if she understood the map, but there was no right, just meadows to all sides, a low stone wall beside them, a metal fence ahead. She turned the now-creased paper, making sure she was orienting correctly, while Aakash walked up to the fence to take a picture of the mountain. Then Deepa located the turn: a stile, hidden by the thick wall stones, led onto a small path along a farm building whose facade was patched in layers, a palimpsest, record of its own epochs. The path led onto a narrow, paved road, but, before long, they turned off into the woods once more.

The children had grown quiet when they exited the first patch of woodland onto the high rim. To their left, the valley plummeted in swales, between pastures and conifer stands. *The myriad greens of the world*—where had P read that? They emerged alongside a river that resembled many they knew in Arkansas, shallow and unhurried, and the kids exclaimed when they saw a cave ahead.

They were Arkansas kids in this way, loved them a cave, Aakash especially, who took the lead, MacGyvering his iPhone to keep both hands free without a headlamp, testing the depths of the still pools on the cave floor. P watched them go in, then waited on the bridge, watching a couple of busy fishermen in hip waders below. She took a picture of a weird sculpture just outside the cave: a tonsured monk in robe and sandals, with a slightly shorter man (they were both short) in boots strapped crisscross up to his knees and holding a walking stick. The men were carved in grayed and striated wood; the monk had laid a hand on the hiker's shoulder to convince or encourage him but they looked past each other as they talked and were also ignoring a wooden dog holding a doggy smile intent on them both.

The kids were gone a long time and P was proud of their spirit of adventure until she was suddenly seized with anxiety and went to go shout into the cave. Just then they emerged, giving off an air of repressed exhilaration, teenagers never wanting to show they were excited.

"It goes back a fair ways," Aakash said. One of his shoes was wet.

"We had to crawl," said Deepa, excluding her mom from the People of the Cave.

They resumed their walk, on the road now, the heat mounting.

"It reminded me of a video I saw about a spelunker," Aakash told them. "He tried to get through a narrow opening in this cave he was exploring and got stuck upside down." P and Deepa laughed in horror but it wasn't a funny story. "They couldn't get him out. Over a hundred people participated in the rescue attempt. They brought in equipment but I think the pulleys came out of the wall. It's called the Nutty Putty Cave, in Utah, because the walls are some kind of soft, I don't know, clay or something. He was in his twenties but died within twenty-four hours, maybe an aneurism? Or, no, his heart couldn't keep up the work, trying to pump the blood away from his head." He was telling the story as he walked jauntily up the road, not looking at them. "They closed up the cave, buried him there, because it was too dangerous to even try to get the body out."

It was a horrible story but also a window onto Aakash's internet and segued into a conversation where they all weighed certain adventures against their attendant risks. P was getting to know her kids differently, away from home, away from Mac and his domineering ways.

★ ★ ★

Halfway to the monastery from the Beau-Lieu, the monks' friends and champions had set up a museum in some formerly grand alpine manor. First, you serpentined through rooms ordered by a monk's segmented day: rising toward midnight to do a solo prayer before gathering with his brethren for lauds and matins; back in his room, saying the "mother's prayer"—a prayer in his mother tongue, a prayer to Christ's mother, who is also his mother. He returns to sleep in the box of his bunk; he rises again around 6:30 for more prayer, reading and reflection, work. Around noon, he eats a simple meal deposited through a slot in the door of his cell. He tends his garden. He prays again, alone and with his community. He eats an even smaller meal. He prays again in community. He sleeps.

The schedule was poetry; the museum rooms its prosody. P looked inside the box bed, inhaled its tangy wood smell, examined the tiny study, the dishes, the icons and tunics, items and trappings laid out with care so that those who wanted could trace, feel, hear the quotidian monastic villanelle. The museum's other half displayed huge aerial drawings of Carthusian monasteries around the world and the tools and materials of their industries—distilling, brickmaking, printing.

Before returning to the monastery path, P sat in the replica garden. Beside her, a lizard ran down a morning-glory-covered wall and emerged to sun on a rock.

The night before, she had brought a book to her own solitary supper. A tasty meal, a good book—*The Charterhouse of Parma*, in the Richard Howard translation. Who knew Stendhal was so lively? Even in the before-times with Hamish, she had considered a restaurant meal alone with a novel to be one of the great pleasures. It became an even rarer luxury during the kids' demanding infancy and toddlerhood. When had the gloss gone off?

She loved having her days alone to daydream and note-take, no demands to overwrite her thoughts. But when work was done, these days, she craved the relief and distractions of her family, the people she not only loved but liked best, their jokes and debates, the pressure and constancy.

Midday sun warmed her skin against cool alpine air. Other visitors passed through the museum behind her. What were Mat and the kids doing back in Paris? She checked her phone: nothing. She could text them but the signal was weak and is that really what she was here to do?

She found herself recalling a ritual she instituted with the children that year Mat was in New York City. On weekends when he didn't visit, she started what she called "slumber parties"—both kids sleeping over in her bed. In a different marriage, they might have co-slept, but Mat had forbidden it, saying it would be terrible for them as a couple: no sleep, no sex. She had given in—he was right—so the "slumber parties" were temporary and subversive, a way to forestall their longing for him.

It was a king bed, plenty of room, but the kids squirmed and squeaked all night, rotating like windmills, elbows and knees poking her like they had inside the womb. She got no sleep at all, which should have put her in a terrible state. Instead, she felt strangely transported, drifting in voluptuous half-dreams amid the perfume of child-slumber, like baking bread, despite occasional little farts.

She would lie with her eyes open, watching the room's subtly changing light and the kids' shifting positions in the bed. She had amazing thoughts she couldn't recall the next day. Evanescent time's flickering shadow-play—she was alive to the present as almost never.

No one else would, could, be what she was to them; no one else could even see into the contents of that irreplicable intimacy, mother and child. The children themselves couldn't see it; they took it for granted, if you did it right.

But what about the intimacy of husband and wife? That, you couldn't take for granted. But she and Mat had arrived into a new place.

He had kept Nikhil and Saro in Arkansas through the fall, bringing them and her parents for the holidays. Her parents had gone back; he and the kids were staying through the remainder of the academic year, sharing a tiny Montmartre flat, Nik and Saro doing virtual school as she and Mat worked, all four of them hot-desking between sofa and kitchen table and the one actual desk. They were having a wonderful time and it was no wonder she needed a break and even more annoying that, now that she had wrested herself away, she missed them, just as, all through the fall, she had missed them.

She couldn't remember when or how she and Mat had decided on this plan. It was as though it sorted itself out under the pandemic's peaceful, despairing blanket. They all emerged and the way forward was clear. She'd felt a fresh tenderness for him since acknowledging her own need—or desire, who knows—for marriage and for him specifically, a feeling that had only grown through those lonely, glorious months alone in Paris before the three of them tumbled back into her life, her space.

She and Mat still bickered and quibbled: two alphas with kids, together almost 24-7. But P understood herself differently now, and found the (humbling, mutual) spaces cleared between them more interesting than the calcification of yore.

Also: such a relief to be out of Arkansas for a bit. Yes, they would return, but the pandemic's best lesson was that the future was a new country, the present an eternal no-man's-land keeping it always out of sight.

She exited the museum past the ticket sellers, two young women who bid her farewell with secretive, near-excessive joviality: a short one with twinkling eyes who looked South Asian and a tall one with milky white skin and half of a blond mustache perched over one side of her mouth. They chattered as the glass door eased itself shut behind her and P thought, as she had with so many people, that she would never know their stories.

★ ★ ★

It had been so stressful to leave Mac, and P was almost euphorically relieved to have done it. She never did return to sleeping with him, but clung to the life raft of her red chaise longue, bobbing on a sea of possibility toward an unknown horizon. Their own bed felt definitively hostile, associated now with breathless panics and sleeps of sweaty oblivion.

Thus they waited out the winter in détente. Mac didn't ask her about her nocturnal absence and she volunteered nothing. She didn't acknowledge it, perhaps because of the pandemic's muting effects on time, change, decisions, perhaps because they were cordial. But she could see in retrospect the emotional and logistical architecture of the marriage's dissolution.

The October day tenure applications were due was also the deadline for sabbaticals. She had not planned to apply—their plan had always been to synch up, but that couldn't happen until Mac was tenured, and she had been eligible for a few years now. So she spoke to her department head and hastily put together an application for a semester at the Sorbonne to translate a

Mauritian novelist who'd written two seminal early books in and about Paris in the fifties before immigrating to live in Saguenay, Quebec. There, he worked for the last twenty years of his life on an epic unfinished novel that a Canadian academic publisher now wanted to publish as an annotated volume and had asked her to translate.

The justifying ligatures for travel were loose but the bar was low: if pushed, she would have to admit she didn't really *need* to go to Paris for the project, but they wouldn't deny her the research leave for that reason. She was productive. She would use the time well. She deserved it.

She had to say in her application that it was contingent on the pandemic lifting, which was a huge contingency, and she didn't tell Mac she'd applied, vaguely reasoning to herself that there was no point until and unless it was approved.

But there had to be a conversation eventually—what exactly had happened or was happening with his tenure bid?—and as Mac failed to initiate it, P's anger at him grew. For all his enlightened bluster, he was too afraid to talk with the people closest to him about the things that mattered most, meekly hoping she'd creep back into their room, their marriage, maybe hoping things would go back to the way they were.

January arrived and brought the vaccine. Magic bullet? P went alone to get her shot. When she mentioned it to the kids that night at dinner, they asked Mac if he had gotten his and he said no. He didn't say he had an appointment. The kids didn't think to query and P was afraid to. Her best guess was that the obstacle was organizational and not philosophical, but better not to ask.

She learned in early December that her research leave had been approved, but it was still far from clear if or when she would be able to leave the country, so she kept the information to herself for the time being. Mac should have learned around that time whether he'd cleared the tenure hurdle at the college level—he should have known weeks if not months earlier whether his departments had approved him—but when she worked up the courage to ask, he waved a hand around as if chopping at undergrowth and muttered something like *it's complicated.*

She didn't ask again until spring, when things were cautiously starting to open up, everyone still masked and distancing but filling shops once more, even teenagers getting their first doses. She was putting away their grocery order and thinking about starting dinner when he came in, mask around his chin, with two panniers full of groceries, enclouded by the air of preoccupation that signaled his intention to cook.

As he pulled out bottles of rosé, she asked, "Special occasion?" He frowned. "No."

The question was out before she clocked that she was asking it. "Any news on the tenure front?"

"This godforsaken place and its romance with the twentieth century!" He slapped steaks onto the counter. It seemed she was getting her own supper, then, as the family's lone non-meat-eater. "I knew from the start there'd be nothing good in Arkansas."

"The U of A's great for what I do," she pointed out, randomly. Beside the point.

"It's different for me."

"Boldly going where no man has gone before," she said, toasting him.

An eye-flicker suggested that he'd registered her tone but he had too much momentum to swerve.

"I'm after something bigger. You just go along to get along, don't ruffle the water."

He was searching for one of his gadgets and didn't see her look grow stony. She took her glass of wine into the living room because there was no use arguing with him, then wondered if her avoidance proved his point.

It was true that the university's default mode was inertia, but the program she taught in had a translation track because a white man had the idea to start one. Hiring Mac was innovative: he'd been brought on to carve a path. But he was supposed to indicate that path by publishing, and he hadn't. He liked industry: the continual ego-strokes of results reports, the dinners, the meetings, the visits. Writing up those results for academic journals took discipline, a tolerance for invisibility and collaboration, some of his least favorite things. Plus his teaching evals were uneven, with a little coterie of students who adored him and the rest feeling excluded. (P had read between the lines of his vocal complaints, until recently, when she opened his computer and read the evaluations themselves.) In addition to which, he'd alienated more than a couple of influential colleagues.

Why would she ruffle the water? She had most of what she wanted. Why would anyone, pre-tenure? It was a white man's luxury to think that was a prerogative.

She'd been wavering on her plan, but this steeled her to pull the trigger.

Six weeks later, she received an email from a private detective with a file of photos attached: Mac taking photos from behind a pillar in the law school; Mac taking photos from behind a stack in the library; Mac taking photos from behind a car in the parking lot of the co-op. She checked the date on the parking lot pictures against her own record: she had surreptitiously started the location-sharing feature on his phone and created a table where she logged his movements and her own. It wasn't hard: she didn't go that many places. She now confirmed that he had likely followed her to the co-op, was likely taking pics of her.

That feeling she had in Arkansas, of being visible and vulnerable: she thought it was the rarity of women of color in her town or campus. What was Mac doing? Did he want to possess her or was he keeping her safe? The stalking had not affected her choices or movements in any way she was aware of, but she still felt he was trying to pickpocket her: trying to steal something—like her autonomy, or her right to invisibility, or her nylon sockettes—without her knowing.

The detective's photos were not great but they were good enough. Mac was recognizable. It helped that he wore his mask under his nose, a style she'd heard referred to as the new manspreading, ha ha. It left more of his face exposed.

She chose nine of the photos to send for printing, nine four by sixes. Then, on a summer day when he'd said he was going to his office but she could see on her phone that he hadn't, she asked the receptionist to unlock his door. P'd prepared an alibi, that she had a surprise for Mac. It wasn't a lie, but the receptionist apparently couldn't care less.

P arranged the prints on his desk in a three-by-three grid, co-op photo in the center. She had brought Blu Tack and pinned them in place on the desk so that her arrangement had some kind of permanence, looked more deliberate. He wouldn't be able to just sweep them off with an arm in panic or disgust.

He acted no different when he came home that night, and she guessed he hadn't made it to his office, a guess she felt affirmed two days later, when he came home late, missing dinner, not even responding to her text querying him before they started eating. He came in quietly, ashen, barely responded to her questions, crept off to bed. Had he even guessed it was her? He never said anything about it and neither did she.

But she had to talk to him about her own plans at some point. An old grad school friend, now at the Sorbonne, who had written her a letter of invitation, had also vetted a sunny Montmartre apartment for her and the kids. When their school ended, she showed Aakash and Deepa pictures of the flat as a way of starting a conversation.

That had been tough. They didn't know what they were looking at, just that it was pretty. She explained that she was going to Paris from January to May and that they had the option to join her, but that it would mean doing school virtually.

They hesitated. Aakash had gotten vaccinated in time to attend the last month of school; Deepa took a chance on returning around the same time since everyone else was. They were done with staying home, so it was a tough call, but they both ultimately decided they'd rather attend virtually to get the time in Paris than stay back with Mac in Arkansas.

"So Dad's not coming?" Aakash had asked. Deepa glanced at him then trained her look back on P, waiting.

P took a breath. "Honestly, I don't know. He's not really talking to me about his plans, so I went ahead and made my own."

They looked old and young and very still. P waited for more questions: *are you guys breaking up?* But they didn't ask. They didn't want to know more than they needed to, and this, too, moved P toward a decision.

In late June, perhaps ten days after Mac found the photos, after he'd had plenty of time, plenty of opportunity, to talk to her if he wanted, on a day when both kids had gone to the pool with their friends, she made tall, icy glasses of sweet tea with lemon and asked him to sit with her on their deck.

He took a sip. "You're leaving."

Finally. "I'm spending the spring in Paris. The kids have said they want to come with me." She caught her breath. "What are your plans?"

"I don't know yet." He was looking at his hands on the beading glass.

"Do you have teaching this year?"

"No."

Okay, then. "Income?"

"I'm lining up contracts."

"Well, you can stay in the house until I get back next summer, but then we need to make arrangements."

"That's it?" He finally looked at her.

"Is there something else you want to say?" Her body was vibrating, not nerves, not even indignation, but as if a second self writhed within her skin.

"We've been together twenty years!"

Why did people always think that was a reason to stay instead of a reason to cut and run?

Now it was spring and France and she was traveling alone with her kids for the first time, finding it easy and pleasant. She would learn in time that there were more ways to think about her marriage than she ever would have guessed, ever-unfolding multiform theories about Mac, about her, about them. The reins of some of those theories were held by her demons of self-loathing; others were in her own hands. If theories were horses, scholars would ride.

Well, watch her: Deepa had found out about guided horseback treks to more distant mountains within the range and easily convinced P to book one. Tomorrow, they would ride, all three.

Now, she felt a rising excitement as they walked onto the wide, worn path to the monastery. Alongside them, the vertical cut to the road exposed root systems in low relief like maps of the earth's understories. She pointed it out to the kids, who were more interested in negotiating the contents of their packed lunches. She understood: they didn't share her fascinations with this obscure place. She was still glad to have them along. She didn't need to talk to them; she could keep what she saw and thought to herself. It's not as though she was alone.

★ ★ ★

She sat on a rock in the meadow beside La Grande Chartreuse. The meadow's steep ascent let her see all the roofs on all the buildings within the monastery's walls; its walls blocked her from seeing anything else. The low repeating arcade of the monks' cells; the bell towers, small and large; the angular relations of black roofs to white stone echoing the mountains' own rocky shades and slopes. She sensed the monks moving within their private architecture, indifferent as nature to her and the others stopping by for all their many private reasons. Why do we use *monastic* to mean solitary when monastic life is inherently communal?

A bell started to ring. P watched its back and forth movement in one of the largest towers and imagined the monk below, ecstatic, teenage, freshly tonsured, faintly homesick.

She knew that staying home in Arkansas might have been a truer homage to the Carthusians, which meant she had to admit that wasn't what she was doing here.

She'd wanted to be in the place where chartreuse came into being, she thought, but why? The color had existed for as long as there had been light, as long as there had been a spectrum—it wasn't a species, evolving from a before to an after. But it wasn't *chartreuse* until the monks made it so, a Wittgensteinian problematic that P pretended was resolvable by a return to origins.

It put her in mind of a recent Maria Stepanova memoir, *In Memory of Memory*, translated by the poet Sasha Dugdale, an episode where the author gets the address of the house where her great-grandfather was born and goes there for the first time. It's now a shoe shop, but as she enters the yard, she is flooded with intuitive recognition, the sense that the house is answering the questions that brought her. *I remembered everything beneath the high windows with such a sense of heightened native precision that I seemed to know how it had all been, in this, our, place, how we had lived and why we had left. The yard put its arms around me in an embrace...*

A week or so later, the colleague who'd given her the address calls her up sheepishly to apologize—he'd gotten it wrong. It was the correct street, but not the right house.

And that, says Stepanova, *is just about everything I know about memory.*

Was that what P was doing, conjuring connections? Manufacturing memories of a place she could never go, visiting an ancestral village that wouldn't meet her eye? Maybe. Except the monks were still making Chartreuse, down within those walls, invisibly. They had been forced out and had returned and again forced out and again returned, implacable as the tides.

She couldn't see chartreuse here. But she could sense its—real or fictional, material or metaphoric, objective or subjective—presence.

It was the idea of chartreuse, *beyond the visible.*

It was an excuse, like any other, to leave home.

ACKNOWLEDGMENTS

GRATITUDE TO

- many dear colleagues, neighbors, students and friends in Fayetteville, AR and Montreal, QC, for community and more.
- Shana Gold for an invaluable early reading.
- Kaveh Bassiri and Kimia Tabib, whose story forms the spine of Mehrzad and Minsha's. Mehrzad's best lines were Kaveh's first.
- Fennec and Jake, chickens and snakes, Pebble, Spike and the whole pet parade, for making yourselves at home.
- Deena Aziz and Shelley Tepperman, for serious levity.
- Bhuvana Viswanathan and S. P. Viswanathan, for coming along for the ride.
- Anjali Singh, agent, and Celia Blue Johnson, editor, for making it seem I wrote this book just for them.
- Ravi Brock and Mira Brock, for being.
- Geoff Brock, for generosity, brio, ever-renewing good humor and Last Words.

ABOUT THE AUTHOR

Padma Viswanathan is a Canadian-American writer and translator whose novels have been published in eight countries and shortlisted for the PEN USA Prize, the Scotiabank Giller Prize, and others. Her most recent book is *Like Every Form of Love: A Memoir of Friendship and True Crime*. Viswanathan's short fiction, essays and translations have appeared in *Granta*, *The Boston Review*, *BRICK*, and elsewhere. Her full-length translations include *São Bernardo*, by Brazilian novelist Graciliano Ramos, and *Where We Stand* by philosopher Djamila Ribeiro. She is Professor of Creative Writing at the University of Arkansas—Fayetteville, where she is Founding Director of the *Arkansas International* Writer-at-Risk Residency Program.

TWO NOTES ON THE TYPE

The text of *The Charterhouse of Padma* has been set in Garamond Premier. It is the creation of Robert Slimbach based upon designs and cuts of the original work of Claude Garamond he viewed in Antwerp, Belgium in 1994. He worked extensively on the family. It was released by Adobe in 2005.

Claude Garamond's own roman letters were designed in his own Paris foundry. Modeled upon the roman of Aldus Manutius, it became the standard by the end of the 18th century. Garamond's cuts are still holding strong today.

The text of *The Charterhouse of Padma* has also been been set in Mr. Eaves Sans Book. It was brought to life by Zuzana Licko for Emigre Graphics, in 2009. Mr. Eaves is officially the companion sans serif to a modern classic called Mrs. Eaves.

Book Design and Composition by Brooke Koven